Namita Waikar was born in Mumbai in 1961. She studied Biochemistry at the University of Mumbai. Namita is managing editor of the People's Archive of Rural India (PARI), where she leads and writes for the Grindmill Songs Project and oversees its translations programme.

She is also a partner in a chemistry databases firm in Pune, which is the culmination of her work experience as a biochemist and a software project manager.

This is her first novel.

THE
LONG MARCH

Namita Waikar

SPEAKING
TIGER

SPEAKING TIGER PUBLISHING PVT. LTD
4381/4, Ansari Road, Daryaganj
New Delhi 110002

First published in India by Speaking Tiger in paperback 2018
Copyright © Namita Waikar 2018

ISBN: 978-93-88326-31-5
eISBN: 978-93-88070-78-2

10 9 8 7 6 5 4 3 2 1

Typeset in Sabon Roman by SŪRYA, New Delhi
Printed at Sanat Printers, Kundli

For
Aai and Baba

'Democracy is the art and science of mobilizing the entire physical, economic and spiritual resources of various sections of people in service of the common good of all.'

—Mohandas K. Gandhi

CONTENTS

1

BUNDLES OF FIREWOOD AND FISTFULS OF FODDER

It was the day after the education minister in Delhi had declared a policy change in school curricula. The teacher of the school in Sonsawali village wrote the news headline of his choice from the day's newspaper on the blackboard with a half-inch piece of white chalk:

'Geography Is More Important Than History'.

The children raised their eyebrows and gestured 'what' at each other in silence. As the teacher underlined the sentence and said it aloud, the older boys and girls hid their confusion in smiles while the younger ones wondered what it meant. The students of Classes 1 to 4 squatted together in uneven rows, on the floor of the single room that formed the primary school. The only teacher they had cycled three miles every morning from his home in Wardha town. He told the children to repeat the headline after him. After a few times, they were able to say it on their own. Then he asked, 'Does anyone know why geography is more important than history?'

A boy volunteered: 'Sir, Gandhiji said so.' The others giggled.

A few students implored the teacher for the answer and others joined in the chorus: 'Sir, sir, you tell us, you tell us. Sir, sir, you tell us.'

The framed photograph of Gandhiji hanging above the blackboard with a slight tilt to the left would have been witness to the answer. But a man entered the classroom just at that moment and whispered into the teacher's ear. There had been a death in the village. The class was dismissed, and the children ran home.

But one boy had not forgotten the teacher's question, and he quizzed his uncle that night, 'Vikram kaka, do you know why geography is more important than history?'

The young man stared at the night sky.

'Do you know the answer, kaka? Do you?'

Vikram Sonare often allowed his nephew to share the rope cot at night outside their hut and knew the boy would not shut up unless he gave him some answer.

'It is because geography is about land and trees, rivers and dams, whereas history is about wars and killings and records of what happened in the past.'

The boy didn't really understand the explanation but it sounded intelligent enough, and soon he fell asleep. But his question kept Vikram awake long into the night, thinking about the recent incidents that had occurred in his village and the neighbouring ones. The deaths of so many farmers, like the one today, had agitated him. How could a man take his own life? He was unable to come to terms with it. Vikram slid off the cot and paced up and down the narrow mud path between his hut and the others. He thought of his own parents toiling in the fields. His memories of them since childhood were the same. There wasn't a day when they were not working in the fields or gathering firewood or performing some task or the other, from morning till sunset. Even now, they let him help on their farm only when he had no classes. They wanted him to complete his education and not leave it unfinished like his brother. Vikram knew that his elder brother Vishwas and their father had taken loans from the bank to pay for cotton seeds, fertilizers and pesticides. Last week, a messenger from the bank had come to remind them of the repayment schedule and the amount that was overdue. When his father requested for more time to make the next instalment, the man retorted, 'I cannot do anything. Why borrow money if you can't pay it back? Come to the bank and speak to the manager.'

Vikram threw himself back on the cot. He had watched his father plead with folded hands, nearly touching the man's feet, begging for more time. He wanted to rush to his father and stop him from prostrating. But he didn't. He felt powerless. His brother stood next to their father, his face downcast.

Vikram tossed and turned, trying to rid himself of that memory, the humiliation. But it played over and over again. After hours of restlessness, his body lay still from exhaustion.

Inside the hut was the rest of the Sonare family: Vikram's mother, Kashibai; his father Kailashnath; brother Vishwas; and Vishwas's wife, Surekha, who was expecting their second child. A curtain made out of an old sari hung on a string separated the two couples, contriving a semblance of privacy. As the night edged towards dawn, Kashibai woke up reflecting on what she had told her husband yesterday:

'Don't trouble yourself like this and make your own

life miserable. Is everything in our hands? We will work harder than before, we will do more work, and if even that does not give us what we wish for, we still have our family, our life. It is a wonderful life. We have one daughter and she is married into a good family. She may live twenty-five miles away but she is happy, and that is enough. Our sons, Vishwas and Vikram, are as good as gold. Vishwas has grown so big and strong. He does odd jobs in the town and is dutiful and helps us during the sowing and harvesting seasons. Our daughter-in-law, Surekha, is also not bad. She cooks well, helps me on the farm and is a good mother to our grandson, Nilesh, who is like a little diamond. We are expecting another grandchild soon too. Vikram is bright and studying on a scholarship. He is a little hot-tempered, but he is young and so clever, one can forgive him his faults. He will surely do something big. We have all the happiness in the world. We have always been strong, our hands and legs still function just the same as when we were younger. We will work. Crops will grow. We will earn money and repay the loans and have more food. Everything will be good, everything will be fine.'

Kashibai stifled a yawn and turned on her side to look at her husband, but he was not there. Standing up, she gathered her loose hair, and tucked it into a bun. Her slim body was agile, even at fifty-five years of age. She quickly rolled up their thin bedding and stacked it against the wall of the hut beside the small pile of items that constituted nearly all of their possessions. Flicking aside the ragged curtain at the entrance, she walked out, adjusting her much worn-out cotton sari's pallu over her head, surveying the still-dark sky. As she moved nimbly through the village, the sky began to lighten and the chirping of birds rose to a loud symphony. Morning sounds escaped from the neighbouring huts.

Forty families lived in Sonsawali village, which could be reached by a road off the highway emerging from Wardha. The road trickled into a thin dirt lane that ran between the fields. Shakti Provisions, a tiny shop, was at the entrance of the village. It provided the villagers lentils, rice, cooking oil, spices, sugar, tea; all the ingredients for making paan—betel leaves, betel nuts, lime, kattha and tobacco tins; soap, shampoo sachets, 'Really Fair and Very Lovely' cream, talcum powder, toothpaste, packets of bindis, hair oil, tiny boxes of Eyetex Kajal, combs, hand mirrors and rope. Behind the shop was the narrowest lane in the village that led to an even smaller shop with a board that advertised, 'tobacco, cigarettes, bidis, fertilizer, pesticide, rope'. Above the list was the shop's English name—Ideal Farm Essantiel.

Readjusting the sari over her head, Kashibai peered around the shops. But her husband was not to be seen anywhere. She hastened to the cowshed. He was not there either. Just as she turned to leave, her eyes darted back, catching sight of something at the deep end of the little enclosure. Toes... Feet...? Her husband's familiar gnarled feet! She called out to him, 'Aaa....ho...!' and the next instant shouted out to her son, 'Vishwaa...aas!' as she ran inside. She felt her heart thumping, the beats filling her ears. He was on the ground, stretched out near a pile of hay. Next to him was a can of pesticide. Hands at his sides, palms open, he lay lifeless. His eyes were closed and his head was turned a little away towards the wall of the cowshed. Kailashnath's ashen face was vacant of the worries that had pinched it the night before.

Vishwas and Surekha came running into the cowshed. Followed by Nilesh, who was rubbing his running nose on the sleeve of his T-shirt, a birthday gift from his grandfather from last year. On seeing her father-in-law on the ground, Surekha silently took Nilesh out of the cowshed, tears streaming down her cheeks. Vishwas crouched next to his father. He picked up a scroll of paper that seemed to have rolled out of his father's open palm. It was a stamp paper. A hundred-rupee, non-judicial stamp paper. A letter on the stamp paper was addressed to the village sarpanch, the tehsildar, the district magistrate, the Chief Minister of Maharashtra, the Agriculture Minister, the Prime Minister, and the President of India...surely, at least one of the recipients would listen to his plea:

> Please take note of my plight. I had taken a loan of Rs 45,000 from the Status Bank of India. I cannot repay the loan or the interest because there has been no rain again this year and my crop has failed a second time. The people from the bank have come to our house three times to ask us to repay the debt. They will come again to ask my wife, my son, and my daughter-in-law to pay the loan amounts that they have also taken. Please spare them any harassment. If they get a good harvest and are able to repay, they will clear the debt. We are not bad people. We do not want to swindle money from the bank. But if we just do not make enough money to repay the loan, then I request you to give us more time or waive the loan. I do not want my family to meet the same fate as mine. Please let them live in peace.

The villagers gathered and crowded in the cowshed. Kashibai's eyes were dry. Only one thought occupied her mind: his worries were all over and now she had both his and her share of worrying to do. Before her tearless eyes, all she could see was her family: Vikram and Vishwas, little Nilesh, Surekha and the one growing in her womb. Kashibai must now worry alone for all of them. She was head of the family now and they were all her responsibility.

She walked out of the cowshed towards their farm. For over an hour she let her feet take her forward. The sun was shining brightly by the time she reached their fields. They had no land of their own in the beginning. She and her husband had worked as labourers, earning ten to twelve rupees each day in the fields of Raghunath Pawar, a rich farmer who owned vast tracts of land. For many years, after the work on the fields was done, Kashibai had gathered twigs of firewood from the adjoining forest every day—risking her life often, for the forest was known to be home to poisonous snakes, wild boar, and even some jungle cats. She would sell the bundles of firewood in their village for two rupees apiece. She would also pluck grasses to sell in fistfuls as fodder to other farmers for their cows and bullocks. Ten paise for a fistful; a hundred fistfuls got her ten rupees in a day. Sometimes her husband would also join her and they would get two large bundles of firewood and a heavy load of fodder. Paise by paise, rupee by rupee, their savings grew over the next five to six years and they were able to buy a small farm of eight acres near the forest. It came cheap because it was away from the village, on the edge of a forest, and it was barren land. Kashibai and her husband had bought this farm ten years ago, such as it was. But it was their own; they had cared for it and grown jowar. The crops grew well in the second year of sowing and the couple had reaped the sorghum grains, a fruit of their incessant sweat and toil. Keeping some for themselves, they sold the rest to Shakti Provisions in the beginning. But now, the crop had changed to cotton and they sold the produce to a trader in the town.

She wanted to ask her husband, *Did you get tired so quickly of all the work and the hard life? Did you not enjoy it as much as I did?* For, at the end of the day, the hard floor of their hut welcomed them like the softest bed on earth. As soon as their backs touched it, they fell asleep, waking up each morning to the same difficult yet beautiful life.

She wanted to ask him, 'Did you get tired of it so soon?'

Sitting on the ground among the tall grasses, Kashibai recalled the good times they had since they bought their land: the sowing, the harvesting and the piles of grain that left her with a sense of great achievement each time they saw the crop flourishing in front of their eyes. Her daughter's wedding and the tearful separation as she left for another village with her groom and new family was a big milestone, that was followed soon by the birth of their first grandchild, a girl. Those were good times.

Their troubles began when they started to grow cotton instead of sorghum. The cost of seeds went up, as did the expense of fertilizers and pesticides. And now, they had to spend money to buy food. The loans from the bank and the debts began to pile up as the crops started failing year after year. One year, they were eaten by worms; the next year there was no rain. But her son Vishwas's wedding and the birth of little Nilesh a year later brought some happiness. Oh! Such happy occasions. Hardships and disappointments marred those years, but as Kashibai reminisced over the joyous times, her fingers dug into the dry earth, her only mute support. A slow stream of tears finally escaped her and she covered her mouth with her pallu to muffle her sobs.

For three days, the villagers of Sonsawali mourned the death of Kailashnath Sonare as per the ritual. Men sat quietly in groups and women cried and whispered, cried some more and talked. Was it quick when it came? Was it slow and painful? Did he have regrets at the end? There were no answers to these questions, for the empty can of pesticide lying next to him was the only witness to his death. It gave him the death he wanted. But who cared about Kailashnath Sonare's death besides his family and the villagers? It was not as if he was the first farmer to give up his life and embrace death. Was there anyone who would tell his story? Were there people who would care to listen?

Two months later, a stranger came to the village. It was early morning. People had yet to leave for the fields. The man reached the house of the Sonare family and asked if he might speak to them. Vishwas invited him inside. Kashibai pulled her pallu over her head and returned his namaste. He was alone, dressed in a simple ironed white shirt and dusty brown pants. Vishwas offered him a seat by spreading a woven chatai on the floor. Vikram lurked near the entrance. He had not spoken a word since his father's death. The visitor sat cross-legged on the mat and, after an awkward silence, he turned to Vishwas.

'I am very sorry to hear of your father's demise.' He looked at Kashibai to include her in his condolences and repeated, 'I am very sorry to hear it.' She looked down and covered her mouth. After a respectful silence, the man continued, 'Is it alright if I ask you a few questions?'

'Are you from the government?'

'No, no. I am just a patrakar. I have a few questions and I would like to write down some things in my notebook. Is that alright with you?' Kashibai nodded in assent and the man brought out what looked like a school notebook.

'When did he die?'

Vishwas gave the date.

'How? What happened?'

'He drank pesticide.'

The reporter was quiet for some seconds. The silence was broken by a teenage boy who rushed into the hut, shouting. 'Vishwas kaka, come and see, my father is at that tree!'

A chill enveloped the room. Kashibai was the first to stand up. Vishwas took the boy outside. The reporter shut his notebook and followed them out as the boy ran towards a small crowd facing the tree. More men arrived, women followed, and children ran ahead. For a long silent moment, everyone had turned their gaze upwards. Then the hum of women crying grew and one voice broke into a wail. The reporter stood in the blazing sun. His camera hung from his shoulder, his dark eyes ablaze. People watched as the police arrived. The dead man was untied and brought down.

Vikram walked away from the villagers and wandered around the whole day. Towards evening, he walked down the narrow lane into the forest adjoining their farm. With his back against a tree, he picked up a stone and threw it into the growing darkness. Birds scattered and a flutter of wings filled the air. He threw another stone and another and another until there were none left on the ground near him and everything in his line of vision blurred. He sat down and rested against a tree. Cradling his face, he let the tears stream out. His voice grew hoarse after a long, pathetic wail of grief. The creatures of the forest listened, their own sounds growing fainter.

2

VIKRAM SONARE

When he was nine, Vikram would sit with his mother as she tied small bundles of grass to sell as cattle fodder. She talked to him while her hands made swift work. Her uncle, Dadoji, had told her stories when she was a child, every day a different one. Most of them were made up but some were tellings of real incidents. From this bottomless chest of tales Kashibai would fetch one and tell it to her son.

'"Dadoji, tell us what happened in Mahad," we would sit around in a huddle and ask him. I was small then. But I remember every word he said:

'"Babasaheb was giving a speech in the hall. And we listened to him enraptured. He told us to fight. Fight for your rights, he said. Be strong and give up dirty habits. There were other big people present there who also told us to be bold and fight for our rights."'

'What are our rights, Aai?' asked Vikram.

'We are equal to everyone else, we are equal citizens in this country.'

'But who says we are not?'

'Nobody says it. But they behave that way. They treat us as less than human.'

'But what happened in Mahad?'

'There was a public water tank there, it is still there in Mahad, in the centre of the town. People like us were not allowed to drink water from the tank, the Chavdar Taley. Babasaheb led the march, others followed him. And he broke the rule and drank water from the tank. Some upper-caste people did not like it and threw stones at them.'

'And then?'

'It took another thirty years or may be a little more for the law to tell everyone that a public source of water is open to all and no one can be prevented from drinking water from it... But our problems are not over, not at all over. They say Babasaheb has written many books. When you grow up, Vikram, you must read all the books. You will understand everything. That is why your father and I want you children to study. Will you remember, Vikram? Or will you forget?'

'I will remember, Aai.'

'Remember what?'

'To read all his books.'

'Which books?'

'Babasaheb's books.'

'Alright, my good boy, now help me put this bundle on my head.'

'This is so heavy Aai, but the grass is so light.'

'Yes, yes, when many small small things come together they become big and heavy. Always remember that.'

As they walked out of the fields on to a mud lane, Kashibai spotted two cyclists from a distance. She told her son to move on to her right. Vikram turned around to look at them when he heard the two young men talk loudly. He didn't understand what they were saying. His mother told him to keep his eyes straight ahead but he couldn't resist turning around again and again as they got closer until he got a heavy slap on the back of his head from one of the men. He stumbled and looked up at his mother who was using all the strength she could to hold on to her head load. The taller one among the two men grabbed the string that held the bundle and pulled it hard. It loosened the load and the smaller bundles within it fell in all directions on the ground.

Vikram stared at the backs of the men cycling away from them. There was no sound more cruel to the nine-year-old boy than their laughter, which seemed to get louder and louder for him, even though it was receding. He wanted to chase after them, pull them down from their bicycles and fight them with his clenched fists.

Kashibai was gathering the bundles and called out to him, 'Help me tie this bundle again. Don't bother about them, they are big people.'

'Like the people who threw stones in Mahad at Babasaheb and others?'

Kashibai looked up at her son's face and recognized the rage. Her own anger was buried deep, out of habit. But it was still an effort to keep calm.

'Somewhat like them, but let's hurry home now, it will soon get dark.'

Through his college years in Wardha, Vikram tried to look for books on Ambedkar and books written by him in his college library. They were not easy to find. And he couldn't issue the books in the reference section. The two cupboardful of books at the Agricultural Technology Institute included some of the works of Dr Ambedkar. One of them was a thin book with a red cover entitled *Annihilation of Caste*. Vikram had borrowed it within days of his joining the institute as a data-entry operator. He read the book multiple times and noted some lines in his notebook:

> The emancipation of the mind and the soul is a necessary preliminary for the political expansion of the people.
>
> Religion, social status and property are all sources of power and authority which one man has, to control the liberty of another.
>
> Can you have economic reform without first bringing about a reform of the social order?

As his reading progressed, he noted down his thoughts in a diary:

> It is alright that a man who makes pots is called a potter and a man who gives haircuts a barber. But why should it follow that their children get involved in the same occupation?
>
> It is alright if some children decide to take up the same occupation as their parents. But why should a community engaged in an occupation be ostracized from the rest of society? Why should society be divided on the basis of such occupations which have become the monstrosity called caste? How can one break and destroy this centuries-old 'tradition'? For it must be destroyed to build a society that respects each individual and where everyone is equal. Where no one is more privileged than the other. Economic equality or some semblance of it is possible only if we are all socially equal.

3

MALLIKA

Mallika Joshi had decided to come back to Bombay. She had to. It was the only way to stop her parents from searching for a 'suitable husband' for her. The candidates they shortlisted were getting progressively worse. And the rejections more and more severe.

She had entered the ladies' compartment of a local at Andheri after letting almost all the other women board first. As there was no seat left vacant, she stood between two rows of women who sat facing each other. Right in front of her sat a plump young woman wearing a short skirt and T-shirt. Pulling at the clinging top and blowing air down her chest, she turned to her neighbours saying, 'Curse this Bombay weather. No rickshaw ready to come to the station from my house. Walking, walking I came! At least I reached on time, but look at me, men, all sweaty and sticky.' Then looking at the others chatting around her, she continued, 'What men, morning morning you all are sharing domestic sorrows?'

Seated next to her was a woman in her thirties dressed in a purple-and-black sari with a zari border, sporting a bindi on her forehead that matched her sari. She spoke so loudly that the others fell silent to listen.

'You know, yesterday, Mr Daftari called me to his desk.'

At the mention of that name, the women around her giggled but shushed each other, all ears for what was to follow.

'He said, "Tell your friend, Ruby, not to wear those tight mini-skirts. It is a distraction for all the staff." There were irrepressible snickers as she continued. 'I was telling Ruby, "You know what we should do one day? We'll all wear swimsuits to office with wraparound skirts over them. Oh, and stilletoes, the sleekest ones. When we reach office, we can throw away the skirts. All tense, all tense, all of them will be tense, even all the oldies!"' The women around her convulsed with laughter. Relentless, she continued, 'Their wives will call us up next day and thank us, "Oh God, after so long, after so long, thank you so much, thank you, thank you,' they'll say."' The whole compartment reverberated with raucous laughter. Mallika wished she had had a book in hand to hide her embarrassment.

Soon the train was close to Churchgate and Mallika stood at the edge of the train, the sliver of space from below darkly beckoning her. She looked up and let the breeze blow over her face. A huge crowd of women was waiting impatiently behind her to reach Churchgate and get on with the day's work. Elbows dug into her back, ejecting her onto the moving platform. Taken by surprise, she ran instinctively. As the train snaked to a stop, others tumbled out and the woman in the brown sari was beside her again. They had been sitting next to each other for a part of the journey from Andheri. Mallika had noticed her scribbling in a small diary while counting on her fingers, probably making a note of sundry expenses. Then she had opened an even smaller prayer book and read through it. The flowers in her hair, a gajra of the sweet mogras that were in season just before summer, had filled the air with their strong scent.

It was 9:30 a.m. Just half an hour till her interview appointment, so she sped up. It was peak time and men from other compartments brushed past aggressively. The woman in brown lifted her pleats in order to avoid soiling the sari; her feet jutting out of worn-out leather chappals, the chipped pink nail paint defying the dullness of her footwear. Mallika found the movement of legs marching around her dizzying. Why am I staring at people's feet? she wondered and raised her head. Soon the woman overtook her. Dodging the men and women around her, she rushed into the swarm crossing the road, just before the policeman blew the whistle and pulled up a rope separating the footpath from the road. Mallika waited behind the rope along with the others and watched the black-and-yellow taxis whizz past along with other cars and BEST buses. People looked at their wristwatches every few seconds, as if that would make time move faster. The policeman blew his whistle again and released the rope, trampling it into a fresh coating of dirt.

Mallika crossed Veer Nariman Road and tried to catch a glimpse of the sea some distance away to her right, where the road met Marine Drive. Walking towards the bus stop next to the Oval Maidan, she saw the woman in the brown sari, way ahead of her.

Drops of sweat were trickling down her back in a tiny stream. At Eros cinema, she checked for approaching buses and spotted No. 86 speeding towards the stop. She ran but the double-decker sped past her. She kept running and wondered if she should give up. Men hanging out from the footboard of the bus turned their heads in unison and watched her.

The bus halted, spilling out a crowd onto the street. People tried to get in and out at the same time. Hoping that would hold the bus longer, she kept running and noticed the brown-sari woman glancing at her as she got in. She was just two feet away when the bus began to move. She ran faster and stretched out her hand and, holding onto a bar, jumped into the moving bus. There was too much of a crowd on the footboard. The bus moved faster and she felt her head and torso get thrown back as it made a swift turn. Catch the arm of the man just in front of you, she told herself, but resisted touching a stranger. For a moment, her grip loosened and her fingers slipped from the bar. Arms in the air, she screamed. I am going to die, she thought. The man ahead of her turned around so slowly, it seemed deliberate.

When she opened her eyes a little while later, she found people staring at her. Her head was leaning against someone. She jerked upright. It was the woman in the brown sari. She said something, but Mallika couldn't hear her. Everyone in the bus seemed to be talking at once.

'She is lucky she didn't fall out.'

'I thought she tried to jump out.'

'No, no, she was trying to jump inside when the bus was moving. She could have caught the next bus, no? Why take a risk like this?'

'What happened, what happened?'

'What's happening? Is she unconscious? Nice way to get a seat in the bus.'

Mallika wiped her face.

'Water? Do you want water?' This time Mallika heard her, the woman in the brown sari, and drank a little water from the bottle she held out.

'Thank you...'

'I'm Sudha Bhatkar. What is your name?'

'Mallika. Thank you for the water.'

'You should thank the man who saved you. You were falling and suddenly fainted, when he caught you and brought you inside. So loudly you screamed!'

Mallika looked around and asked, 'Can you show me who it was?'

Sudha surveyed the bus and, shaking her head, clicked her tongue. 'He's not there now. Maybe he got down from the bus at the previous stop.'

Trying to recollect the man's face, Mallika vaguely remembered a shirt. 'Was the man wearing a checked shirt? Cream-and-red checks?'

'Yes, yes, he was. Young man, he was. Very fair, and curly, curly hair.'

Mallika didn't know what to say.

Thanking Sudha again as they got off at Nariman Point, Mallika walked across to the tall building on the other side. It was almost 9:50 a.m. and she was a good ten minutes early for her appointment. The office of Care People was on the fourteenth floor of Mittal Tower A. Inside the lift, she pressed her back against the cool metallic wall. Her mind went blank as at least three people stared at her, two men and a woman. The office was at the end of the corridor. A fifty-year-old, or possibly older, receptionist peered at Mallika through her spectacles and indicated a chair for her to sit on while she spoke on the phone. Two large wooden frames were stacked against one wall behind the woman's desk. They must be paintings, Mallika thought, resisting the urge to pull them out to look.

'Yes, may I help you?' the receptionist asked as she put down the phone.

'I've come for an interview. My name is Mallika Joshi.' She handed over a thin folder to the receptionist. Her resume barely ran to two pages, while photocopies of college marksheets and degree certificates added some importance to the file.

'Please be seated,' she smiled and disappeared behind a door.

Returning moments later, she said, 'You'll have to wait for some time, maybe half an hour. You could come back later, if you prefer, or wait here.'

'I'll wait here.'

Glad to sit undisturbed, she relaxed for the first time that morning.

She had some newspaper cuttings of paying guest advertisements in her handbag, which she pulled out to take a quick look. There was one near Five Gardens area in Matunga that she had highlighted. Mallika was lucky that her friend Ritu had offered to let her stay with her till she could find a job and a paying-guest room. Otherwise, it would have been too difficult to convince her folks to let her return to Mumbai. Ritu and Mallika had lost contact over the last six years. But had gotten back in touch with the help of some common friends. It felt good to be back in Mumbai. In spite of the heat and constant sweating, Mallika felt free here somehow. It was also a good thing

that the last 'boy' she 'saw' decided to reject her, God
bless him. Had he not done that, she'd have probably been
saddled with an unworthy marriage. After being rejected
ten times already, she'd lost the right to reject anyone, so
said her mother. As it is, at twenty-six she was already too
old, according to her mother, to find a nice boy. All the
nice boys were twenty-six or -seven or -eight at the most,
seeking fair and beautiful girls of twenty-four or younger.
Some months ago, at twenty-five, she was still a borderline
case, but all that changed after her twenty-sixth birthday.
Her status shifted from 'unmarried' to 'spinster', her brother
had jested. Mallika's mother had scolded him, thinking she'd
feel hurt. But she needn't have bothered. All that had been
over and done with with the very first rejection.

She still remembered the day quite vividly. It was on the
day of the last paper of her MA final exams. After throwing
her books and bag on the table in her room, Mallika had
gone to the kitchen for a glass of water, hoping to crash on
her bed afterwards for at least a month. Instead, her mother
made her sit at the dining table. She said there were some
people coming over that evening. 'Fine, let them come.' She
wasn't interested. But something was definitely going on
as her mother's face had that seldom-occurring expression,
hovering between excitement and calm. It turned out that
the guests that evening were a boy and his parents who
were coming to 'look' at her. Before Mallika could voice
any protests about arranged marriages, her mother had
produced a photograph and she missed a heartbeat. Taking
the photograph from her, she looked at him again. He was
very handsome. Soon her brother and father returned home
and there was no time left for a nap. She was completely

caught up in the idea of meeting this boy, and getting ready for the 'event' until finally, the doorbell announced their arrival. The boy was even more attractive in person. Mallika tried to look at him without seeming to do so. That same night the Joshi household got a phone call, informing them that the boy had said no. Mallika was the only one who was surprised. Her parents weren't. She remembered later that the boy had flinched on seeing her—her spectacles rather. It had not occurred to Mallika even once that the boy would reject her, simply because in that split-second of seeing the photograph for the first time, she was convinced that her life was going to change dramatically.

Mallika cried herself to sleep that night. All her plans of enjoying the long-awaited vacation crumbled. More meetings followed, some with horrible-looking boys. She endured the ritual every time without interest or an attempt to generate any. At one point her mother suggested switching to contact lenses. She refused to part with her specs for any man. Rather have my specs than a husband, Mallika told her mother with borrowed bravado. Her brother supported her, and for once he was not jesting. She started taking English tuitions for some children in the neighbourhood just to pass time. Her MA results had not been spectacular either.

One fine day, Mallika decided to apply for a diploma course in social work at the university. It was a new course, so getting in was easy. Most of the students were girls, who gasped at her having an MA. They were all BAs. There were also a few confused and rather useless boys who seemed to have chanced upon the course.

When Mallika looked at her watch, she realized fifteen minutes had gone by. She desperately needed a job soon and was particularly keen on this one. She had read about Dr Sriram Kasbekar in the newspaper two years ago. He had started Care People with his own money, including all that he had inherited from his parents. He also financed a lot of smaller social service projects and guided smaller organizations in their work. It sounded like just the place to start her career. Besides, it was a productive way of escaping home. She had sent a letter to him and had been called for the interview, quite promptly, to her delight and surprise. Eventually, the receptionist picked up the phone and spoke softly, even Mallika couldn't hear her. Then she told her to go in.

Upon entering the room, Mallika saw a man standing with his back to the door. Tall, grey-haired and slim, his short-sleeved white shirt hung loose over khaki trousers. He turned around and, giving her a half-smile, told her to be seated.

'Sriram Kasbekar.'

'Mallika Joshi.'

They shook hands.

Although his hair was completely grey, Dr Kasbekar could not have been more than thirty-five. He leafed through Mallika's resume and certificates while she sat stiffly in a straight-backed chair, going over the highlights in her mind. Age: 26 years. Qualifications: MA History, PG Diploma in Social Work. Specialization: Community Development. Experience: A two-month community development project.

He looked up at her.

'Well, Mallika. May I call you Mallika?'

'Yes...Dr Kasbekar.'

He paused and played with a glass paperweight on

the table. The transparent blob was filled with colourful specks. He stared at the twirling colours, seeming to have forgotten Mallika's presence. Then he looked up, focusing his eyes on hers.

His voice was deep and mellow, almost velvet-like.

'You don't really have any experience. This kind of work involves co-ordinating with many people and organizations. We are not a grassroots outfit. Our core strength is raising funds and securing resources for other social sector organizations that work directly on projects in areas of health and education.'

She thought for a moment before answering. 'Well, I worked on a project last summer with a group of women who made dry snacks to earn a modest income, and they also learned to read and write at the adult literacy class that I took for them thrice a week. I realize that I don't have the required experience, but I am willing to learn. And, given a chance, I would do my best to meet your expectations.' Even she felt as if she'd been parroting one of those how-to-succeed-at-an-interview books. He was silent, so she continued. 'Maybe you could hire me on a temporary basis for a few months and evaluate me after that?'

He frowned, and she thought she shouldn't have opened her mouth. She remembered her brother telling her that men don't like to be told what to do, especially by women. It was dreadful to think of what he might say next.

'Tell me, Mallika, how and when did you think of doing social work, and why?'

He sat back in his chair, the frown gone.

Mallika had rehearsed several points for such a question, but all her preparation faded away and she said whatever came to mind.

'I did fairly well in school but did not finish anywhere near the top of the class. I have not been ambitious about any of the much-sought-after professions, like medicine, engineering or architecture. Sometime in my early youth I thought that I...that I wanted to serve the poor...and the oppressed. At first my parents were disappointed at my lack of ambition. But they accepted it later...after they realized how serious I was about social work.'

She was embarrassed. It sounded made up even to her own ears.

'So, Madam Mallika, not knowing what else to do with your life, you decided to do social work,' Sriram declared. 'Do you think people like you are needed by the poor? People who have no idea about what else to do with themselves? Or do you think you should have more of an inclination to do something for the "poor and oppressed", as you call them? Does it make you feel good, or perhaps great even, that you will do something for them? Does it make you feel like God that these people have no choice but to accept what you give them? Is that a big boost to your ego? You want to practise benevolence on the poor and try to acquire some greatness in the eyes of others who don't give a damn about these things? Is that what you are after? Is that what you are looking for?'

Mallika was stunned, speechless. Was he mocking her? He was mocking her.

'Well, do you have anything to say or are you going to just sit there staring at me?'

She opened her mouth, but no words came out. She felt her hands shaking. Somehow, she managed to stand up, gather her file from the table and, mumbling a 'thank you', walked out of the room. She made a feeble attempt to return the receptionist's smile.

Once outside the building, she walked aimlessly for a while, finally drifting into the first restaurant that appeared before her, uncertain of how she arrived there, which road she had walked on or which direction she had taken. It was the first time she'd gone alone to a restaurant. Sunlight streamed in through the windows into the darkened, dingy place. She sat at a shaded table, not too far from the entrance. Without looking at the waiter, she ordered a Thums-up. She gripped the chilled bottle and, feeling the dirt on it, looked about for something to wipe her sticky palms with. The portly cashier of the Udupi restaurant, whose eyes continuously scanned the room, noticed her. 'Napkane, NAPKAA...YNE,' he barked at one of the boys. A waiter came sprinting and slid a plate with paper napkins arranged in a circular pattern on the table. Picking up the dirt-rag from his shoulder, he wiped the bottle and scurried back inside. There were just three other people in the restaurant. One man sat alone, the other two were together. The rest of the ten-odd tables were empty but looked recently used. Her eyes fell on a transparent box on the manager's table with 'Care People' written on it. In it were a few coins and some rupee notes. Two rupees, five rupees, a solitary ten-rupee note and many one-rupee notes. All the notes had one thing in common: they were old, soiled, torn and tattered, some of them cellotaped in the centre. Too decrepit to be accepted by anyone, she thought. So people had dumped them into the donation box. It would be too much trouble to get them exchanged for good ones from a bank. Too much trouble! Better to give them for charity, an easy way out. The problem of disposing the soiled notes disappeared with the added benefit of making one feel benevolent.

Then it struck her that Sriram Kasbekar had accused her of wanting to do the very same thing. Her chest hurt as she sipped continuously, in an effort to stop her lips from quivering. She blinked hard several times to fight back the hot tears that threatened to spill out at any moment. She realized she had not given any serious thought to what she wanted to do. And she had Sriram Kasbekar to blame for it. Or thank. And yet, she could not stop the overwhelming feeling of resentment, which completely overrode the awe and admiration she had felt for him earlier.

Covering her mouth to silence a burp, she walked to the counter and paid the bill. On her way out, she pulled out a fresh-looking ten-rupee note from her wallet and shoved it into the donation box.

4

THE PHOTOGRAPHER

It was 9 p.m. when Mallika reached home.

'Oh, hello, come in,' Shantanu, Ritu's husband, said as they walked inside.

Soon Ritu came to her and said, 'Come, come, what took you so long? I was getting worried you had lost your way again.'

'No, I just got delayed'.

Ritu urged her to have dinner right away and introduced her to a few of the guests. Mallika excused herself, promising Ritu she would join them in a few minutes. She had forgotten all about the party and wanted only to stay in the guest room, but for Ritu's sake she would have to join the party, at least for a while. For the time being, she escaped from everyone, shutting the door on them. The guest room in Ritu's flat had become her room since she had arrived, thanks to Ritu and her husband Shantanu's generosity. They said she could stay as long as she wanted, for a year even. But Mallika knew she should get a job soon and look for a place of her own. She wanted to lie down and sleep but her mind kept going back to the events of the day.

After leaving the Udupi restaurant, she had walked all
the way to Gateway of India and stared at the dark water
of the sea beating against the boulders and the parapet.
Leaning against the parapet, which, having soaked up the
heat of the day, felt warm, she looked far out to the water
sparkling in the sunlight. It looked blue out there, not black
as it did closer to the shore. But then a stream of street
vendors began to pester her with their wares: 'Madam this',
'Didi that', 'Behenji this', 'Sister that'. They pushed strings
of beads, hairclips, roasted chana-moongphalli, gajras, ice
lollies, whistles, caps, and other whatnots into her face. So
she turned away and headed to the Jehangir Art Gallery.
No one will disturb me here, she thought. Fifteen or so
people, in pairs and groups, their faces turned to the walls,
examined and discussed the artworks in hushed tones. She
stared at the paintings. By the time she had circled the
entire room, her feet ached and her stomach felt empty.
She walked into Samovar adjacent to the art gallery and sat
at the only empty table in the restaurant. She ordered the
first thing that registered from the blurred menu card. The
waiter promptly brought her a sandwich and salted lassi. She
took a sip of the lassi. Overcome by pensiveness, she asked
herself the same questions that Sriram Kasbekar had asked
her that morning. Had he just asked them to rattle her and
make her angry, she wondered. He's probably laughing at
me right now. The interview had turned out differently than
she thought. It had been short. It had been serious, but not
the way she had imagined it would be. She wanted to stop
feeling sorry for herself but couldn't stop dwelling on it.

  She wandered aimlessly for the rest of the afternoon:
looking at shop windows, leafing through second-hand

books and magazines for sale on the footpaths. She bought a newspaper, intending to sit somewhere and read. I should be going back to Ritu's place, she reminded herself, but continued to drift. She sat on a park bench and read the paper. The city went about its work.

After an hour of sitting on the bench, she walked to the Sterling theatre. There was a children's movie on and she went in amidst the crowd of kids and parents. It was one of those documentaries with all kinds of animals and cheeky narration that only the parents could really enjoy. The children were noisy and happy just watching the antics of the animals. After the film ended, she walked around a little more and then took a bus to Churchgate station, where she waited for a train. At Andheri station she got a bus immediately, but still lost her way to Ritu's place from the bus stop. After about ten minutes of confusion, she realized she'd got off too early. So she took an autorickshaw and reached Ritu's.

After having a quick bath, Mallika slipped into a pale green chikan salwar kurta. It was not really party wear but it would have to do. She would have preferred to stay in her room and not mingle with strangers. But for Ritu's sake, she went back to the hall where the chatter had subsided into the clink of spoons on plates. She spotted Preeti in the far corner of the room. Like Preeti, Ritu was also an old classmate from school. But it had always been Ritu and Mallika who played together. Preeti rarely joined them unless it happened to be a big group of all the children playing together.

Suddenly Mallika realized how hungry she was and decided to eat first and catch up with Preeti later. She served herself some pulao, bhindi fry, dal and salad and sat in a chair in a corner of the room, hoping no one would notice her. A small lamp with a violet-coloured shade sat on the corner table and she was glad to think that her face would be lost in its shadows. But her solitude did not last long.

'Hello there,' greeted a stranger and sat in the empty chair next to Mallika's. 'Iyer,' he said and raised his glass.

She managed a smile, which was met with: 'So you want to be left alone. You should've moved away this empty chair. Since you didn't do that, you shall now be punished with my company.' Mallika laughed a little and, for the moment, forgot that she wanted to blend in with the shadows. 'Hello, hello, hello. It's good to see you again today, well and alive. Do you often jump onto moving buses?'

Mallika sat up, startled to be spoken to in such a familiar tone. And then the words of that woman in the brown sari, Sudha, rang in her ears as she saw before her what Sudha had described as a 'young man...very fair with curly, curly hair'. She pushed back her specs and, for a moment, she was nonplussed and said nothing, before remembering her manners. She fumbled as she looked for words to thank him appropriately.

'Thanks. Thanks so much for...this morning... I don't know how it happened...not enough words to express... thanks, again.'

'Given the circumstances, I can't be saying "You're welcome" or "My pleasure", can I?'

'Sorry, I didn't get your name,' she continued fumbling.

'The name's Iyer.'

'Iyer?'

'Yes'

'Hey, have you two met?' Ritu asked, having suddenly appeared out of nowhere.

'Well, she was about to reveal a secret to me and you had to spoil it.'

'Oh dear, am I interrupting something?'

'You might as well introduce us,' said Iyer, without taking his eyes off Mallika's face, which she noticed.

'Mallika, this is Iyer. Iyer, meet Mallika, a close friend from schooldays. She's staying with us right now.'

'Mallika Joshi,' she added, needlessly.

'Nobody seems to know Iyer's first name,' teased Ritu. 'You can try finding out though. Who knows? He may tell you.' She left them and went to the door to speak to a couple leaving the party.

'Well, it's nice to meet you,' said Iyer, suddenly sounding formal. 'You are staying here with Ritu and Shantanu?'

'Yes. That is, until I find a paying guest accommodation, after I get a job.'

'What sort of job?'

'Social work.'

'Oh, I cannot help you there. But maybe I could help you find accomodation.'

'Thanks. You have done a lot for me today.'

'Maybe I'll give you a call tomorrow. It is getting late. I should be leaving, too...unless you would like to go for a drive just now.'

She stared at him, not knowing what to say and wondering if she had heard him right.

'Hey, don't look so worried. I was just joking!'

He stood up and was about to go away but lingered, with his hands in his pockets.

Trying to bring the conversation back to normal, she asked, 'So, do you work with Shantanu?'

'Well, kind of. I am a photographer and sometimes I work for his ad agency.'

She was silent again, at a loss for words, when his jovial mode returned.

'I drive a jeep. It's more fun to jump into than speeding double-deckers. But...maybe another time.'

'Yes,' she said, tentatively, feeling inadequate and acutely conscious of her glasses. She felt them growing bigger and covering her entire face. She pushed them back again to drive away such thoughts. Too much was happening in one day and she wanted to be back in her room.

'Where were you going this morning?'

'For an interview. Like I said, I'm looking for a job.'

'Oh yeah,' he said.

All the guests had left except Preeti, who came towards them just then. Waving her fingers at Mallika, all rings and long red nails, she began, 'Mallika, it's so good to see you. We should get together sometime and catch up.' Iyer looked from her to Mallika and back. Mallika realized he was still holding her hand and slowly slipped it out of his hand.

'You two know each other?' he asked.

'Yeah, way back from school,' answered Preeti.

Then, taking his arm, she tugged at it. 'You are supposed to drop me home. Come on, it's getting late.'

'I don't remember making any such promise, but if you say so,' said Iyer.

Preeti gave him a playful punch on his arm. Saying their goodbyes to Ritu and Shantanu, they walked out of the door, Preeti still firmly grasping onto him. As Ritu pushed the front door to shut it, Iyer popped his head back in and called out, 'Mallika, I'll give you a call tomorrow morning,' leaving her with his smile.

Mallika noticed Shantanu relaxing on the sofa, his arm going around Ritu as she slid close to him and rested her head on his shoulder. Leaving the happy couple to themselves, she bid goodnight.

Lying on the bed, she realized just how tired she was from all the day's aimless walking. Her legs felt heavy. Switching off the light, she crept into bed. Remembering those words again, 'very fair, curly, curly hair', she thought of Iyer and instantly recalled Preeti gripping his arm. Was that a warning to her? She then wondered if she should feel flattered that someone as attractive and glamourous as Preeti might be threatened by her. But then, suddenly, Dr Sriram Kasbekar's questions barged into her mind again. Curse you, she wanted to say to him. She yawned and turned on her side. Tomorrow I will start again. Look at other opportunities, she decided. But the questions kept coming back to her. Her sleep was punctuated with strange dreams that night and, when she woke up, the images and words were so vivid that she recorded them in her diary:

Twice I went there
Riding on a bus
Alighting each time near a temple, crowded
Inside the temple, a big courtyard
With muck everywhere that
Some women were trying to clean
It only moved from here to there
Not getting cleared

Outside was a narrow lane
Always covered with a stampede
First it was the pigs
Then came the dogs
Then cows and
Buffaloes followed
And then finally came schoolchildren
In blue and white uniforms
They did not pass the temple by:
Entered into the Clean Courtyard.

Something without stirred and woke me up
The stampede city was my mind in dream-state.

5

THE SECOND CALL

After breakfast that morning, the telephone rang and Shantanu passed the cordless to Mallika while continuing to look through the papers.

'It's for you,' he said, neglecting to tell her who the caller was. It couldn't be Iyer this early in the morning, could it? Mallika took the phone with some trepidation.

'Hello?'

'Hello, is that Mallika?'

'Yes, this is Mallika speaking.'

'I'm Mrs Wadia from Care People. Can you come again to our office today?'

'Yes, but...' she felt a little reluctant after what happened there yesterday.

'Just a moment, Dr Kasbekar would like to speak to you.' Mallika waited while Mrs Wadia got him on the line.

'Good morning, Mallika. Sriram here.'

'Hello, good morning.' Mallika tried to keep a neutral tone; she was not going to let him know how rattled she still felt, nor was she going to make it easier for him.

'I would like to discuss a job opportunity with you...

not something that you are currently looking for but it is an opening at Care People all the same. Sorry to call you so early in the morning, but can you come in to see me at around eleven or eleven-thirty?'

'Alright,' she said, 'I'll be there.'

'Good, see you then.' The phone clicked.

Soon the phone rang again.

'Hello,' Mallika said tentatively.

'Hi, Mallika! Good morning. Glad to know you were waiting for my call.' It was Iyer this time; she was even more surprised.

'Oh, Iyer, hi. Actually I was just on the phone to...' He laughed so she stopped mid-sentence.

'Hey, so what are you doing today?'

'I am going for another interview, at the same office at Nariman Point that I went to yesterday.'

'I'm going to town, too, so I can drop you there.'

'Isn't it out of the way for you? I can take a bus from Churchgate.'

'Like yesterday?'

They were both quiet for a while. Iyer cleared his throat but waited for Mallika to respond. She felt that he wasn't going to take no for an answer.

Finally, she broke the silence. 'I need to reach there at eleven.'

'Right, I'll pick you up at ten. Does that work?'

'Okay.'

Shantanu glanced up from his papers, an amused grin playing on his face. Ritu, too, was smiling and absentmindedly over-buttering a piece of toast. Shantanu looked at Mallika pointedly and, although he continued to smile, there was a serious note in his voice.

'You know, Mallika, I've known Iyer for some years now. There has always been a string of beautiful girls trying to catch him and pin him down. But this is the first time I've seen a change in the pattern.'

Ritu joined in, 'Be careful, Mallika.'

And they both laughed at the confusion they saw on her face. Mallika felt relieved when Yashoda brought in Shruti, all ready for school in her uniform of white-and-pink checks. She was completely forgotten by Shruti's parents, kissing their pretty little daughter goodbye and generally fussing over her. Yashoda was their live-in maid.

Iyer came promptly as promised. They got into his grey Mahindra jeep. He suggested Mallika put on the seatbelt. She searched for it, first to her right, then to her left.

'Here, let me do that.' Iyer bent over to help her.

It was a moment in slow motion. She thought of the time her maths teacher in school explained the theory of probability. When you toss a coin, what is the probability of getting heads or tails? She had never understood that question, but for some reason it suddenly seemed important, as she felt that Iyer was somehow able to read her thoughts. Mallika tried to keep a straight face. Iyer pulled the belt from over her left shoulder and clicked it shut in its holder on the right side. She let out a long breath.

Quite expectedly, a replay of yesterday's bus event followed. Once again, Mallika thanked Iyer as profusely as she could for saving her from falling off. He said she should thank his mechanic as he had kept the jeep for an additional day of servicing, forcing him to resort to public transport. Iyer kept chatting away the next hour, trying to get to know Mallika.

When they reached Mittal Tower an hour later, he said, 'I'm going out of Bombay for a few days. I'll call you after I return. Keep in touch.'

'Sure. Bye, and thanks for the ride.'

Mallika went up to the Care People office and Mrs Wadia told her to go straight in to see Dr Kasbekar. He was writing something but looked up as Mallika entered the room.

'Please take a chair. Give me just a minute.'

While waiting for Dr Kasbekar, Mallika noticed his clear grey eyes, with some crow's feet at the corners. His forehead, too, was lined. His beard was well trimmed and he was conventionally handsome. I am surrounded by handsome men, Mallika thought; though Iyer was not so much handsome as attractive, especially his large dark eyes, which were only magnified by his long lashes. Sriram put down his pen and turned his attention to Mallika.

'How are you, Mallika?' he asked, stressing on the 'how'.

'Fine, sir, thank you.' She waited for him to bring up her behaviour yesterday.

'Mrs Wadia will be leaving us soon; she informed me recently. I would like you to work in her place if you are willing to take it up.'

'Mrs Wadia?' Mallika asked, surprised.

It turned out that Mrs Wadia was going on long leave for a year to join her children in Canada. Her post would be vacant within a week and Mallika could take it up if she were willing. Mrs Wadia's work involved keeping in touch and corresponding with all the grassroots social-work organizations that Care People financed and co-ordinating meetings between their representatives and Dr Kasbekar. There was also some routine administrative work, filing and the like, that would need to be done.

'After some months, maybe we can hire another person for this position and you could then take up more specific assignments. In the meantime, you can familiarize yourself with the work we do, as you'll come in contact with a lot of different people. You can give me your answer now, or you can take a day to think about it.'

'I can join now,' Mallika said, amazing herself.

Sriram did not show any surprise. 'That's good. I'll ask Mrs Wadia to explain everything to you. When would you like to start?'

'Today, if that's okay.'

'That's fine then. You can spend some time with Mrs Wadia. In the afternoon I can brief you more about our work.' It seemed like the discussion was over. But Mallika lingered.

'The questions you asked me yesterday, I have been thinking about them.'

'That was the intention. To make you think. It is important to understand that when you work in the social sector, the focus should be on finding out what is required, what is needed by the people, and then work towards providing it. Often I have found that people focus more on what they would like to give rather than on what is really necessary.' He smiled through his beard. It was as impersonal as a smile could be, making it obvious that their talk had concluded, but Mallika stood there and continued her questioning, 'Why did you want to do this work?'

'Oh! Quite simple. For very selfish reasons. It's the only thing that makes me happy. I can't imagine doing anything other than social work. But I won't call it that. I think of it as working for myself. Doing what makes me happy.'

As she walked towards the door, Sriram called out. 'Mallika, thank you.'

Mallika smiled and walked to Mrs Wadia's desk. Apart from explaining the work, she also told Mallika a few things about herself.

A week later, Iyer called late in the evening. Mallika tried not to sound surprised or happy. After the first greeting there was a pause, which he finally broke.

'Aren't you going to ask me where I am?'

'You'd said you were going out of Bombay.'

'Don't you want to know where I am?'

'I thought since you didn't say… anyway, where are you?'

'I'm in Kolhapur and tomorrow I will be in Goa. I will return on Sunday.'

'Okay.'

'How was your day?'

'It was good. Oh, I got the job. Not what I'd applied for but it's something of a good start.'

'That's good, congratulations!'

'Thanks.'

'I'll call you when I return on Sunday morning.'

'Yes, do call, I'd like that.' And then he put down the phone without saying goodbye.

It struck Mallika later that Iyer hadn't joked or laughed even once during the conversation. She thought of how his curly hair was a bit long but well kept, of his dark eyes, constant and steady, that kept her pinned to the spot, and the way they lit up when he smiled. She looked at the calendar on the wall and counted the days till Sunday. Four long days. For some reason she thought of Sudha, the woman in the brown sari who had first described him to Mallika. She wondered about her, where she lived and whether they might meet again on the local train some day.

6

TIN BUCKET

Bhikaji Mansion in Jogeshwari was a four-storied building that always had at least three bedsheets hanging from different spots along the edge of the gallery. Watching those bedsheets from above were shirts, blouses, trousers, saris, frocks and shorts that dangled from iron or plastic strings. The walls of the chawl were once painted a bright yellow. Now they were a collage of dingy yellow swathes, patches of cement grey, strips of greenish-black mossy growth, fading handbills and peeling posters. Three sides of this seemingly dilapidated structure embraced a rectangular open space that defined the lives of the residents.

Boys and uncles played cricket here in the evenings and all day on Sundays, except when there was a match to be watched on television. Scooters and bicycles were parked at haphazard angles, blocking people's paths. For weddings, everyone helped decorate the pandal and take it down once the ceremony was over. Girls managed to find some space away from the cricket players to play langdi and tickker-billa, leaving their hopscotch to run home when their mothers yelled out their names or simply appeared in the gallery. Some men played volleyball on Sunday mornings, their sweat-stained baniyans and striped underpants causing utter embarrassment to their teenaged daughters. During the nine nights of Navratri, the space would be strung with colourful lights, buntings and a small stage would be erected for a band. Everyone would dance to the beat of dandiya music, hitting their sticks together to the rhythm of remixed Bollywood hits, far past the approved hours. During Diwali, bits of blown-up paper from burst firecrackers would get scattered on the ground. The coloured water and powders of Holi eventually turned the square into a murky mess.

But life was not always so festive and carefree at Bhikaji Mansion. The open space was often witness to fights among the tenants, usually over the early morning queues for the two water taps on the ground floor. Then there were occasions when everyone would observe a respectful silence, when for one last time, surrounded by grieving men, crying women and confused children, a dead resident shrouded in white cloth and blanketed in yellow and white garlands of flowers, was placed in the centre of the square for the procession to the cremation. By sheer luck and in quiet defiance of known and unknown statistics, the open ground at Bhikaji Mansion had never played host to a fire engine or a police van.

The two parallel sides of the rectangle contained ten kholis each, while the side joining them had seven kholis. With ground plus four floors, there were a hundred and thirty-five kholis in all. Each squarish room was divided by the tenants into two or three smaller rooms by way of wooden partitions or, more commonly, curtains. The number of occupants of each kholi ranged from two to fourteen, depending on the size of the family and any relatives latching on. It was the kind of community where few family secrets remained so for long. The old women of the chawl wielded their authority to examine every newly arrived bride on matters of looks, complexion, dowry, jewellery, child-bearing prospects, and showered her with advice on various conjugal matters. If the bride did not conceive within three months of marriage, they would take it upon themselves to remind her of the importance of giving her husband a child as soon as possible. During such sessions, each of the older women would proudly proclaim how she had produced a child each year for the first four or five years of her marriage.

Sudha had not been spared either. But after nearly a year of not conceiving, the women thought it best to ignore her. There were other young brides to pester. Sudha Bhatkar, the woman in the brown sari who had offered her water bottle to Mallika, lived on the fourth floor of Bhikaji Mansion.

Sudha wakes up at four-thirty each morning without fail and then works like a woman in a trance. It is only at this unearthly hour that she can easily draw water. An hour later, when those on the lower floors start to wake up and draw their own water, it no longer reaches up to the fourth floor. By six, water can be drawn only from the ground floor. Besides, at this early hour she does not have to wait in a queue at the common lavatory. While the water runs, she prepares breakfast, which for today is pohe. She also begins preparing lunch, washing and cutting vegetables for bhaji and mixing wheat flour to make chapattis. Then she washes clothes that she soaks overnight. By the time she finishes all this, it is 6:30 a.m. The sounds of the radio and traffic from the road break the early morning silence. The crows caw, although there is a mysterious randomness to their schedule. Sometimes they do not appear until nearly 8 a.m. That morning, one appeared much earlier. Sudha shooed it from the window ledge as she put water on to boil in the blackened steel pot that had once shined like silver. While the tea water bubbled, she swept the floor clean with a few strokes of the thin broom. She added tea powder and sugar into the boiling water and then swabbed the floor. The house was small enough to clean in the time it takes to make three cups of tea. The strong aroma of tea spread throughout the tiny home. She handed a cup to her father-in-law. Placing a cup of tea on a wooden stool next to the iron bed, Sudha patted her husband's cheek, waking him up. Bed tea for her beloved every morning!

She laid out two porcelain plates of pohe for the men, on the metal table in the front room, garnishing it with a squeeze of lemon and a sprinkling of very finely chopped coriander. Gulping down her tea from a saucer, she ate her own share of breakfast from a small steel bowl and rushed to the tiny bathroom, carved out of the kitchen space, for a quick bath. Her sole ambition in life was to own a flat of her own, an apartment with a big bathroom. Her thoughts do not dwell so much on how many rooms the flat should have or how big the kitchen should be. The single concern, uppermost in her mind, is a large bathroom, where she could bathe for an hour at a stretch. Streaming out from a showerhead would be hot water, just the right temperature. Or maybe there would be a bathtub and a handshower that would pour water gently, like music. She would then reach out for a soft, white towel, dry her hair with it and roll it up on her head. She would have another towel to wipe herself dry before slipping into her baby-pink bathrobe. It was a

fantasy evolved from looking intently, repeatedly and with
fascination at the luxury soap and shampoo advertisements
in *Femina*, a magazine she regularly borrowed from her
office library.

Dhad-dhad, dhad-dhad! The bathroom door shook
violently as someone was banging hard on it, saying, 'Hurry
up, you maharani!'

Sudha was cruelly awoken from her daydream.

'Hurry up!' shouted her husband Ramesh.

'Yes, yes, I'm just finishing,' she lied. In fact, she had
not yet started her bath. She was sitting on one side of a
low wooden stool.

'Can't have a decent bath in this house,' she grumbled
as she burst out of the tiny four-foot-by-three-foot bathroom
after bathing. Ramesh glared at her.

'As if you were living in a palace before marrying me!
You did not even *have* a bathroom in that tiny hellhole of
your village. You used to bathe outside in the open with
well water; no soap, too. You must have smeared yourself
with mud instead.'

Sudha heard him splash water from his head to the floor.
She clicked her tongue as the tin bucket hit the floor a third
time while she dressed in her brown polyester sari. She had
four saris that she considered decent enough to wear to
work. She was saving money to buy two more so that she
wouldn't have to repeat two saris within the same week.
Invariably it was the brown sari that got a double wearing.
It was her favourite, even more so since her nasty-tongued
neighbour, Nayak aunty, had commented, 'It looks very dull
on you,' when in fact, Sudha had noticed her surreptitiously
admiring it only a moment before.

She was almost ready, dabbing a maroon bindi on her forehead when her bathed and cooled-down husband came into their tiny bedroom, partitioned from the front room with thin plywood. He shut the door and stood close behind her, locking her in his arms.

'We'll be late,' Sudha whispered as he squeezed her left breast.

'And he is sitting outside,' she added, referring to her father-in-law. Ramesh had already spotted his father walking to Nayak uncle's side of the long, shared balcony to discuss the news with him.

'Quickly, come on, quickly,' was all he said, moving his hands all over her in a frenzy and untying her sari. Sometime later, Sudha was draping her brown sari for the second time that morning.

It was 8:20 a.m. by the time they picked up the lunch boxes that Sudha had hurriedly packed, and walked out briskly towards the Jogeshwari railway station. Ramesh softly whistled a tune from *Sholay*, while Sudha repeatedly told him to shut up.

'I'm going to be late again. All because of you.'

Ramesh laughed with pleasure and only whistled louder.

'Shut up!' she shouted, exasperated as they flagged down an autorickshaw.

'This is how we waste money and time,' she complained as the driver adjusted the rear-view mirror and turned up the volume of the music that was blaring out the same song from *Sholay*.

Ramesh laughed heartily and put an arm around his wife, which she quickly brushed aside and told the driver to switch off the music. After that they continued in silence. They usually walked the twenty-minute distance to the station, but hired an autorickshaw whenever they were running late, which was quite often. Sudha took a quick sip of water from the bottle in her purse and patted her husband's arm goodbye. Then she ran to the station to catch the train to Churchgate while Ramesh paid the fare and took his time walking to catch a train in the opposite direction to Malad.

7

GULABRAO

Looking up from the broadsheet, Gulabrao acknowledged the tall glass of masala chai brought to him by his manservant. He took a long sip and cleared his throat as a piece of ginger went down it. Spread out on the coffee table was *The Nation's Voice*, the country's second-largest English newspaper. Gulabrao, the Minister of Water Resources in Maharashtra, had just finished reading an opinion column that made an oblique reference to a politician in a land-grabbing case. There was no direct mention of Gulabrao's name but the piece had infuriated him all the same. Especially the line: 'those who govern water resources have extended their arms into acquiring forest land with dubious methods, land that should rightfully be left alone.' He would have had the writer's neck if he could. In fact, he knew the chief editor of the paper personally. But even the chief editor was unable to stop the damn reporter, Bhaskar Prabhu, from making the scathing remarks pointing towards his involvement. The man liked to call himself a rural reporter and wrote about farmers and conditions in the countryside, but more often than not he would stray into other areas, reporting on corruption and irregularities. In the past, Gulabrao had sent one of his men to lure him into his network of cronies. The man came back red-eared from verbal abuse. So, this reporter could not be bought, at least not as easily as several others had been on earlier occasions. Gulabrao decided he would have to try out a different approach to discredit the man in some way.

Leaving the glass of tea on a table, Gulabrao plodded to the anteroom for his daily round of tel malish. The manservant gave him a quick massage with warm oil and left the room. He then arranged his master's clothes and stepped out of the room, reappearing only when required. After getting dressed, Gulabrao popped a pod of cardamom from a small silver platter into his mouth and walked to his white car. The red overhead light glowed as the driver turned on the ignition.

To counter his restlessness, Gulabrao called Uday Dhanraj from his slick new mobile phone. Let's meet today, he told Uday. Saat baje. It was understood that Uday would pass on the message to their other friend, Padmanabh Seth. It was further understood that they would not be meeting at Gulabrao's official government residence, but at the bungalow in Kandivli in suburban Mumbai. They always met in secret, never in public, unless it was at an official or media event where they were present in professional capacities.

Stretched out on black leather chairs that evening, Gulabrao and Uday relished their whiskey on the rocks while Padmanabh sipped his lemon water. Padmanabh was the teetotaller among the three. Gulabrao and Padmanabh chewed on lamb kebabs, while Uday popped roasted cashews and diced carrots. Uday was the vegetarian of the group. And soon Gulabrao spoke about what had been bothering him all day—the latest column by Bhaskar Prabhu.

'Just a poorly paid reporter. Thinks too much of himself. He is talking about the golf course. But he cannot mention my name. He dare not!'

'Do you think we should handle him?'

'No, no, Uday. Just ignore him. Silence is the best rebuke for guys like him. Hurts their ego.'

'Gulabrao saheb, why don't you just buy the newspaper he works for?'

'I already have one that my nephew owns. Don't want another one. Why don't you get someone to buy it, Paddy?'

Padmanabh Seth took a long sip from his lemon water and stretched his legs in midair for a few seconds.

'That's an idea. Let me think about it.'

Gulabrao put his glass down. 'Forget this Bhaskar-taskar. I was watching a game my grandson was playing the other day. I got one for us too. Something called the "Game of Life".'

'Gulabrao, you want us to play children's games now?' laughed Uday as Padmanabh looked on with interest. He caught the serious undercurrent in Gulabrao's expression as he opened a large package.

The game was spread out on the large centre table. And the pair of dice was thrown as their blue, red, and green pieces progressed around the board. Each player had to acquire, sell and sometimes lose different assets on the game board: a home, a school, a library, a bookshop, a farm, a well, a park, a bicycle. While they played, Gulabrao told them what each of those assests stood for. He guided Uday

and Padmanabh in charting their plans for real acquisitions;
real estate in the most expensive areas of South Mumbai, a
new group of independent universities across the country,
media empires, vast tracts of farmland, huge expanses for
oil drilling and refineries, golf courses and automobile
factories. Mining was left open. But they agreed to come to
that later. It was understood that businesses would be set
up in the names of their extended families, close friends and
cronies who would in turn benefit from their many forays.
After a short while, as they relaxed with their last drinks,
Gulabrao said, 'Power is nothing unless you can make it
grow constantly and acquire wealth while doing it.'

The next morning, Gulabrao got a phone call from
a senior official of the Maharashtra state government. A
Parliamentary Committee on agriculture from Delhi was
planning on visiting Yavatmal district in Vidarbha in the
next two days. Eight members from major political parties
were to be part of the team. They would be visiting Hemarja
village as well as the twin villages of Kopardi and Govargaon.
Queen Seeds Inc., the American company, had showcased
all three villages as beneficiaries of their genetically modified
cotton seed that had near total monopoly in India's cotton
sector. The official was aware that Gulabrao's maternal
cousin owned Princess Agroseeds, the Indian arm of Queen
Seeds. Gulabrao thanked the official for this priceless bit of
information, the most vital part of which was that Bhaskar
Prabhu would be accompanying the committee members and
had suggested which villages they should visit.

Gulabrao smiled to himself as he called his cousin about
the visit. He was sure that they could fix the visit for the
benefit of the seed company and discredit Bhaskar Prabhu's

stories. The cousin had already heard of the impending visit and was in panic mode.

'No, no, the visit cannot happen. Not now! Do something, please. Tell me what I should do for you... umm...uh...what you want me to do?'

Gulabrao chuckled as he ended the conversation. Ordering his PA not to interrupt him, he spent the next hour on the phone talking to people all over Nagpur. First, he called his man in the Nagpur subdivision; next, a builder friend in that city; an MP from the opposition, BNP; two MLAs from his own party; and a friend who was the principal of an arts and commerce college. Finally, he called his nephew, the publisher of the Marathi newspaper, *Lokaavaaj*. Now all he needed to do was to wait and watch the events of the following day.

In the meantime in Mumbai, Bhaskar Prabhu ran into an official of the Maharashtra Government at the airport who informed him that the visit to Yavatmal by the parliamentary committee had been cancelled.

Bhaskar called two of his friends who were also expected to be there—Manoj Rathod, leader of the Vidarbha Farmers' Association, and Devdutt Hande, the local reporter. Next, he called Mr Jyotirmay Sen, the MP and Chairman of the Parliamentary Committee, who was getting off his flight at Nagpur.

'Mr Sen, the visit should not be cancelled. All the people, the farmers in those villages will be waiting. They are expecting to see you and the others from the committee.'

'Yes, Bhaskar, let's see tomorrow. The state government cannot direct us. They cannot change our plans. We will go ahead with the visit. Let us see how it goes tomorrow...'

After reaching Nagpur late that night, Bhaskar stayed awake, making phone calls. He rested for an hour before starting off for Yavatmal at 4 a.m.

When he reached the District Collector's office, he found out that the visit had not been cancelled even though only four members of the committee had arrived instead of eight. Mr Sen informed Bhaskar that he had spoken to state authorities and the visit was to happen as planned. The District Collector remarked, 'Sir, you are right, the visit has not been cancelled. But there is a slight change of plan. Instead of visiting Hemarja, Kopardi and Govargaon, we will be going to Purankheda. Farmers from the three villages have already assembled there.'

Bhaskar expected Mr Sen to put his foot down and insist on following the original plan but felt rather disappointed when he meekly said, 'Alright, then, as you say, let's all go to Purankheda.'

The group travelled in three vehicles for the hour-long journey. The visit was not going as Bhaskar had hoped. He really wanted the committee to meet the farmers in those three villages so that they could report the findings in the Parliament session, which was due to start in a few weeks. The whole thing was a washout! While the two men continued talking, Devdutt, who was following them in another car, was busy calling some of his contacts in Purankheda, trying to repair the situation.

At Purankheda, a group of men dressed in crisp new shirts were introduced by the District Collector as farmers who had used the cotton seeds from Queen Seeds and made a success of their farming ventures.

One of the panel members asked, 'Are you all really farmers? You all don't look like farmers!'

'Yes, yes, we are farmers. We have got very good yields of cotton. We were also trained in the proper use of pesticide, farming techniques, and management by Princess Agroseeds and Queen Seeds companies.'

They painted a fairytale picture, ensuring that the committee would go back and furnish an encouraging report about the effects and use of Queen Seeds.

While they were talking, a crowd of people had gathered—Purankheda was more of a small town than a village.

One man in the crowd began without preamble, 'Saheb, those men are not farmers. They are traders. I am a farmer from Hemarja. Why don't you come there? I can take you. So many farmers are expecting you there. They are waiting there for you all.'

The District Collector reprimanded the farmer in Marathi but Mr Sen interrupted him in Hindi.

'Kisan bhai, how far is Hemarja from here?'

'Kyon Saheb, mazaak kar rahen kya? As if you don't know? Just take a short jump from here and you will land in Hemarja.'

Laughter ensued in the crowd as Mr Sen directed the group to get back into their vehicles and ordered, 'Let's go to Hemarja. Kisan bhai, please come with me. What is your name?'

'Govind Bhelke, Saheb.'

The farmer sat between Bhaskar and Mr Sen and issued directions to the driver, who replied in Marathi, 'I know where to go, don't think you are the only one who knows his way around here.'

Seated next to the driver, Devdutt smiled and caught

Bhaskar's eye in the rear-view mirror. They were enjoying the small victory.

At Hemarja, the entire village was out in the street, including the tribal Adivasis and Banjara people and around thirty widows of farmers. A beautiful rangoli in bright colours welcomed the Parliamentary Committee. Bhaskar Prabhu and Devdutt Hande were greeted with namastes by some of the villagers they knew.

The sarpanch made a customary welcome speech and as he began to praise the benefits of Queen cotton seeds, the villagers drowned his voice in protests and forced him to stop.

A woman came forward and spoke directly to Mr Sen, 'Saheb, you must do something for us. We get no rains sometimes, we need proper irrigation. And even when we do get rain, the cost of seeds and fertilizers and also pesticides go up. We cannot recover even our own kharcha. The amount we spend on the crop is much more than what the government pays when they buy our cotton. How can we survive? How do we repay loans? We don't even get enough credit from the banks.'

A young man added, 'Saheb, we are forced to go to the moneylenders who are fleecing us. My father and uncle have both taken their lives in the last five years. I don't even want to be a farmer. It gives us nothing.'

Another man came forward. 'Saheb, I'm Mangal Raut. I was one of the first farmers to use Queen Seeds. I can tell you they are good seeds.'

There was a hush in the gathering.

'For how long have you been using the company's cotton seeds?' one of the committee members asked.

'Five years, sir. I got special training from the company.'

'That's good.'

Mr Sen then turned to the District Collector, who had been ignored all this time, 'How much irrigation do you have in this region?'

'Sir, about two per cent.'

Mr Sen asked the farmer who had just praised the company, 'So with levels of irrigation as low as two per cent, and as an experienced farmer, which seed will you prefer to sow? Queen Seeds or ordinary cotton seeds?'

'Sir, ordinary seeds, because more irrigation is required for Queen Seeds.'

Two of the panel members and a few other people present there sniggered.

A man pushed through the crowds to reach the front, waving sheets of paper in his hand and began shouting at the visitors, 'Saheb, why don't you come to Kopardi and Govargaon? So many farmers are waiting for you there.'

'What is that in your hand?' Mr Sen asked him.

'Saheb, it is a copy of the petition. Signed by seventy farmers from Kopardi and forty-five from Govargaon. More people are signing.'

'Alright. Are you from Kopardi?'

'Yes, saheb.'

'And I'm from Govargaon,' said the man standing next to him.

'So, both of you, please come here and sign that copy of the petition. Give it to me. And send me the original petition when all the signatures are completed.'

The two farmers could not stop grinning as they handed over the petition copy with their signatures on it. Devdutt Hande photographed them.

Mr Sen then continued, 'Now, does anyone here want to talk to us?'

Nearly fifty people moved forward. But the committee had time to listen to only sixteen of them.

Many spoke about the relief packages sent by the Prime Minister and the Chief Minister of Maharashtra. They had received money to dig borewells and could buy pumps at a good discount from a company designated by the government. A man interrupted to add that the agency supplying the pumps was owned by the village moneylender.

'But, saheb, we do not get enough electricity. We get it only for a few hours everyday. So we cannot use the pumps. They are all rusted now.'

The villagers walked with the visitors right up to their vehicles. As the cars were leaving, a bunch of children chased after them shouting, and waving as the visitors waved back at them.

Back in Hemarja, the villagers congratulated themselves. They expected something to come out of this important visit. Surely the committee would report their findings to the Parliament and take the matter further for the cause of the farmers, just as they had promised.

But Govind Bhelke, the farmer who had enabled the members to travel over to the Hemarja from Purankheda, retorted, 'Don't start dreaming that your woes will be over. The Prime Minister visited us three years ago. What happened? Then the young leader from INP party visited us. What happened? We are still crying. And they drive in and drive off in shiny cars.'

At night, Govind Bhelke's wife asked him, 'What made you rush like that to Purankheda? And where is the bicycle?'

'I had to go there to bring the committee to our village. I could not let my friends down.'

'Which friends? You are telling others not to expect much from the visit. Then why did you go?'

'I don't believe much will happen from the committee visit but my friends do—Devdutt and Bhaskar Saheb. I have faith in their belief.'

'And where is the bicycle?'

'Stop asking questions now. I will bring it back tomorrow. I left it with someone in Purankheda.'

Late in the evening back in Mumbai, at his bungalow in Kandivli, Gulabrao smashed a glass in the never-used fireplace. His nephew had informed him on phone of how they had failed in thwarting the visit by the Parliament Committee. Later he tried to console him 'Don't worry, Kaka, we will give a favourable report in *Lokaavaaj* tomorrow.'

8

ANTS AND HUMANS

Miles away from Mumbai, in Sonsawali village, Vikram Sonare was walking to work in the morning. His rubber chappals clapped against his heels, and the dust soiled the edges of his dark trousers. At five feet ten, Vikram was taller than his elder brother Vishwas and among the tallest men in his village. His white shirt strained against his broad shoulders and chest, and the short sleeves flapped in the breeze. As a child, Vikram often played with the other children in the village. But there were times when he would be alone, engrossed in things nobody knew about.

One of his favourite pastimes was to observe ants and their activities, especially the way they carried food, marching soldier-like in a single file. He would try to distract them and disturb their order. Using a thin blade of moist grass sprinkled with a little sugar, he would try to lure away an ant from the middle of a long row marching up a tiny anthill.

One time, an ant approached but turned back. A second one creeped up and then another followed until, slowly, the rest of the ants joined and marched in the direction he had set.

He had been ecstatic at his achievement. That was ten years ago.

Vikram smiled at the recollection of his boyish pursuits as he reached the institute. He was already eagerly waiting for the afternoon. Back at his desk, he jabbed at the keyboard, mechanically entering numbers from the data sheet. He paused to look at the sheet. The column heading was 'Temperature' and he was entering air temperatures taken at different times of the day. He had completed his second year B.Com exams and was now working as a computer operator at the Institute of Agricultural Technology at Sonsawali in Wardha district while awaiting his results.

The advantage of working at the institute was access to the internet. Curiosity about ants led him to seek more information on the insects. His interest was further piqued when he read that ants are part of an order known as hymenoptera and that bees and wasps also belong to the same order. But it was their social structure that set him thinking even more deeply.

Ants live in colonies that may be as small as fifty of predatory insects living in the natural cavities of trees and rocks or they may live in complex organized colonies occupying large territories. These colonies may be inhabited by millions of ants. But the significant point to note is that the larger colonies have a majority of females, wingless and sterile whose purpose is to exist as 'soldiers', or 'workers'. All such complex ant colonies have some fertile males and females called 'drones' and 'queens' living inside them. The ant colonies operate as a unified entity and work together to sustain the colony.

He read the paragraph repeatedly, quite amazed that such a social structure could actually exist amongst insects. It also set him thinking about its similarities with human society. But what stunned him was that while the drones and queens were biologically different from the majority of worker ants, humans were 'equal' creatures physically and yet, most of human society lived like the worker ants, while a privileged few could afford to live like the drones and queens. This line of thinking consumed him completely.

He had forgotten for the moment how much the approaching afternoon had excited him, until he heard footsteps and the pleasant clink of silver anklets. She had brought a friend, a girl who followed her like a shadow. Vikram greeted them with a smile broad enough to hide his displeasure at the unwelcome third party.

Vikram pulled up a chair for Rupali very casually. Her friend was standing by and fidgeting, not knowing what to do. Vikram was supposed to teach Rupali basics about using a computer. He began by explaining basic applications like Word and Excel, which were all new to the eighteen-year-old, two years younger than Vikram. She was thoroughly impressed and the admiration in her eyes pushed Vikram to rush into explaining the Internet and email to her, although he had planned to keep those two lessons for the next day. After a while, Rupali's friend cautioned that it was getting late and that they should leave. Rupali, by now hooked onto the magic of the computer, was in no rush and asked her friend to go ahead as she wanted to stay back. Dismayed, the friend walked away. 'Show me how to search on the internet,' said Rupali, her hands hovering over the keyboard.

Vikram opened the browser and typed *Vidarbha*. Then

she pulled the keyboard back from him abruptly and very slowly typed his name, *Vikram Sonare.* 'You are not famous,' she said.

'No, atleast not yet.'

Gazing at each other, they were lost for a while, until the still-depressed keyboard gave off a loud beep.

'Tomorrow I will show you the Internet and email properly,' said Vikram, running his hand through his thick black hair.

'Okay.'

'Will you come in the afternoon?'

'Yes,' she replied. Her smile reached her doe eyes as she ran home, adjusting the dupatta around her neck and flinging her long thick plait from her shoulder into the air.

Vikram was daydreaming about the next day for a while before going back to his data sheets. He wanted to finish the day's work quickly so that he could freely surf the internet. He had been looking at different government websites. Yesterday he had read a paper by Dr Kabir Rehman that gave suggestions on how to improve the lives of farmers in the country's rain-fed regions where irrigation was almost non-existent. His heart filled with pride at his good fortune, on being able to work at the institute founded by the scientist. He was glad that someone like Dr Rehman had time to think about people like him, living in villages and working on small farms. He searched 'Dr Kabir Rehman' and discovered a news item that read: 'Dr Kabir Rehman's recommendations on agriculture gathering dust.' His joy was shortlived. Then, he searched 'small and marginal farmers' and 'Vidarbha' and found several news items, some of which were distressing. He saved a copy of Dr Kabir Rehman's paper and the news items in a folder. He decided to read them all over the next few days. He was more than aware of the hardships, the loans from banks and moneylenders, and the debts that almost every farmer in his village had incurred, including his own brother, since their father had taken his own life some months ago. But there were many gaps in his knowledge until he began reading, and it all seemed to connect and make sense.

The concluding paragraph of a paper on farmers' suicides stayed with him as he shut down the computer and locked up the room:

> Changes in state policies rarely come without pressures created by mass movements from within the deprived sections of the population. India has had an enviable tradition of farmers' movements, with large scale mobilizations taking place even as late as the 1980s. But today such movements seem to have dried up: large numbers of farmers seem to be taking their lives rather than taking to the streets. And suicide is a cry of desperation rather than a form of social protest. It is this aspect of the situation that is as disturbing as the epidemic of farm suicides that we witness today. The reasons for this lack of protest are not known; and understanding this is as important as understanding the reasons for this rash of needless deaths in the country.

On his rope-cot outside the hut that night, he looked up at the sky filled with stars, but in his mind the words that played over and over again were 'farmers' movements' and 'social protest'. He began recollecting the facts he had read about ants and the parallels he had found with human existence. Was it time for another movement? What would it take to shake up the authorities and convince them to pay attention to their plight? Where did he stand in all this? What could he do? He knew he must do something. The rage that had kindled inside him after his father's suicide had not subsided. He knew something drastic needed to be done. But at the moment he did not know what it was. Perhaps the coming days would bring some answers.

9

LEMONS

It was going to be a hectic day at work. There was a lot of paperwork to go through and many things to check with Mrs Wadia as it was her last day. In two days, she would be flying to Canada. Mallika still struggled to answer the questions Sriram had asked on the first day of the interview, but she had decided to not worry about them too much. She chose to focus on learning from Mrs Wadia and had created a comfortable routine for herself by now. She had to start to look at some paying guest options. She had liked one in the Five Gardens area near Dadar. It seemed very much like what she wanted and the rent was reasonable, too. Iyer had offered to help whenever she planned to shift. There was not that much to move though; all her belongings fit into one suitcase and one handbag.

Mallika and Iyer had met a few times. It was always he who had called. Waiting at the bus stop now, Mallika was wondering if she would call Iyer in case he did not phone for a few days. The bus arrived and since the queue was short, she managed to snag a window seat right in front.

The bus stopped at a traffic signal. Out in the street,

a boy was selling lemons. Neat piles of gleaming yellow spheres were arranged in the wicker basket he held in one hand. In his other hand, were four lemons. 'Dus ka char, dus ka char!' he yelled, the veins of his slim, brown throat bulging out. Who would buy them now, in the morning rush hour, Mallika wondered, when a lady in an autorickshaw handed him twenty rupees for eight of them. Touching the money to his forehead and lips, he thanked the Almighty for his bouni, his first sale of the day, before tucking the proceeds into his pocket. The lady in the autorickshaw said something to the boy. He reluctantly took another lemon from his basket and gave it to her, without complaint. First customers of the day tend to take advantage of vendors keen to avoid marring the first sale of the day with a refusal or an argument, lest it augur bad luck for the rest of the day's business. The lady could have asked for two extra lemons and she still would have got them. As the traffic signal turned from red to green, the boy angled left swiftly to reach the road divider.

Mallika's thoughts went back to the boy. Why was he selling lemons instead of going to school? A day of happiness in his life depended on the fate of those lemons, sold or unsold; each new day began with a basket of fresh stock or maybe some leftovers from the day before.

The bus soon reached Andheri station. The slow train from Andheri to Churchgate took at least three quarters of an hour. Mallika plonked herself into a seat and rested her head against a wall panel. As the train moved, a cool breeze stirred.

Mallika woke up to someone tapping her on the shoulder. It was Sudha Bhatkar. She sat in the seat next to her, took her hand and said, 'How are you? Mallika, no?'

'Yes, I am fine, thanks. How are you, Sudha?'

'I am fine. Just a little worried about getting a loan for a house.'

Her voice dropped and she leaned her head closer to Mallika.

'You know, Mallika, I live in very small kholi in a chawl. I don't like to stay there. I want to buy a flat and for that I need loan. It is not easy to get. But if I do get one, I have made one promise to God.'

'Oh! A vow?' Mallika was not sure why Sudha was telling her all this. So she tried to respond as politely as possible.

'Yes, a vow. I have promised God that I will go to Pandharpur vaari.'

'Vaari?'

'You know...vaari? It is like...ummm. People walk to Pandharpur to visit the Vitthal temple there. It takes twenty days' walking, actually. It will not be easy, but that is the promise I have made. I have not told my husband. He will laugh at me.'

She fell silent then, her thoughts transporting her to some other place.

At Churchgate station they bid goodbye.

When Mallika reached the office, she found Mrs Wadia eagerly waiting for her. Something had come up and she had only two hours to spare at the office before returning home. She had to leave for Canada today instead of three days later. So they hurriedly went over the list of things that they had planned to cover. Dr Kasbekar too joined in as they finished. Mrs Wadia hugged Mallika as they parted and promised to write to her.

Dr Kasbekar returned to his room and Mallika sat in Mrs Wadia's chair. For a moment she drew a blank and didn't know what to do next. Then she heard her name.

'Dr Kasbekar, did you call?'

'Mallika, come in. Sit. Let's not be formal. You can call me Sriram.'

'Alright.'

'We have a meeting this afternoon with the group from Mulund, right? They want to run a mobile school for the children of construction workers. You can go through the plan they have submitted.'

'Yes...Sriram. I'll prepare for the meeting.'

'Good. I'm going out for some time but I will be back before the meeting. So, you think you can hold the fort while I'm gone?'

'I'll try...I mean, yes, I can.'

He smiled and walked out as Mallika went back to her desk to study the plan. Mobile Learning consisted of a group of college students. They had started this programme by pooling in their pocket money with some seed money from a generous patron, who wished to remain anonymous. They owned one van that visited different construction sites in the Mulund and Thane areas on different days of the week. The children of workers at each site were taught basic reading, writing and arithmetic. Mobile Learning provided the study materials for each two-hour class. And they took it back to use at the next stop. They were now looking for more funding to help them improve and expand their services.

Mallika noted down the questions in her mind:

Did they ever intend to enrol the children in regular schools? In what language were the children taught? They probably hailed from different states and may not have a common language. How did Mobile Learning keep track of the children if they moved from one construction site to another? How often did they move? Moving from one site to another with no permanent home seems a daunting prospect.

Mallika wondered how these children adapted. And her thoughts returned to her own search for a home. Soon, she would need to move out of Ritu's place and settle in a paying guest accommodation; a room of her own.

10

MOVING OUT

A heavily pregnant Ritu came into Mallika's room one evening soon after she'd returned from the office.

'Mallika, quick, come with me for a pani puri.'

Mallika was busy packing her bags.

'What?'

'Let's go have pani puri. I've been craving it for the last three days. I must have it. Leave that. Come quick. Your hair is okay. Just come.'

'Should you be eating that roadside stuff?'

'Oh, never mind about that. Let's go before Shantanu turns up.'

Leaving her half-filled luggage and a heap of clothes on the bed, Mallika followed Ritu out of the room and down the staircase. They walked to the shop at the end of the lane. In the daytime, Jai Maharashtra Bhandar did modest business selling roasted peanuts, chana, puffed rice kurmura and spiced gram. But from 3 p.m. onwards, the shop would transform into a wildly popular bhel puri, pani puri and sev puri stall. Hungry men and women returning from office, students from their tuitions, housewives taking a break, all thronged to the shop during the evening. The bhaiyya who generally took the orders noticed Mallika and Ritu approaching and nodded in greeting. Ritu signalled 'two' with her fingers. The man knew that Ritu never ordered anything but the pani puri.

As he prepared the first puri for them, they both stood obediently with their empty plates, like little girls waiting for their share of goodies and sweets. He first served a puri to Ritu and then one to Mallika. The cool spicy water filled their mouths and on the first bite the hot stuffing in the puri hit their tongues, creating a momentary sting that was washed down by the sweet-and-sour mixture of the chutneys and the puri. The taste stayed with them even after they returned home.

The day after their pani puri binge, Ritu delivered a boy. The baby was pre-term but there were no complications. Mallika postponed her move in order to help Ritu out. Shantanu was delighted to have the son he wanted. Mallika stayed with them for two weeks after Nishant was born, and then it was time to say goodbye.

Bags packed and the room cleared of her belongings, Mallika took her leave. Returning from the door one last time to kiss Shruti and Nishant, she looked at the ever silent Yashoda, who gave Mallika one of her rare smiles.

Finally, Iyer arrived and helped Mallika carry the bags to his jeep and they headed to Five Gardens. The owner, Mrs Hattangadi, lived alone in a two-bedroom flat on the first floor. She was to go out that day and had given Mallika a key to let herself in. But when they reached the flat, Mallika was unable to find the key.

'Where's the key? Didn't she give it to you? And where is the old lady? Shouldn't she be here to receive you?'

'The key was here in my purse. I can't find it now.'

They searched the suitcase and bags, but there was no sign of the key. Exasperated and apologetic, Mallika told Iyer she'd take a taxi back to Ritu's place. But Iyer insisted on taking her to his flat at Mahim as it was closer, and wait there till Mrs Hattangadi returned. Mallika was in no mood to refuse or argue. It was too far to go back to Andheri and bother Ritu again. So she left a note for Mrs Hattangadi. Then, with bag and baggage, they trudged back to the jeep. Iyer laughed out loud as he found Mallika scowling.

'Relax, Mallika. It's not that bad. I promise not to eat you!'

Mallika laughed in return and sat back, enjoying the prospect of getting to see where Iyer lived.

They reached the flat in less than half an hour. One part of the large hall in the apartment was crammed with tripods, cameras, lenses, and the walls were covered with photographs. Most were pictures of women, though one wall was reserved for wildlife and looked impressive.

'Did you click all these photos?' Mallika asked Iyer. He looked offended at first, but then patiently went on to tell the story behind each photo.

'I am amazed at how you remember so much about each photo.'

'That's easy. I can recall the details from seeing how good or bad the work is.'

Mallika explored the rest of the flat. There was a small non-functioning kitchen with a little marble countertop and a sink filled with used coffee mugs. In one corner of the large bedroom were a few shirts on hangers. She spotted the cream-and-red checked shirt amongst them. The shirt that saved my life! she thought, reaching out and fondling its soft cottony texture in her palm. It felt like meeting an old friend. When she turned around, she saw Iyer standing there. He came closer and hugged her. For a moment, his embrace was so tight that she could hardly breathe. Her arms went around his back of their own volition.

After a while Iyer released her and with his hands still on her shoulders, looked into her eyes. 'You know, that day, you could have held on to so many of the people standing ahead of you in the bus. It took some courage and a lot of confidence to not do it.'

'Oh!'

'And may I also add that you were immensely foolish not to hold on to me when you could have. I had no choice but to quickly grab you to keep you from falling.'

The phone rang, breaking the spell. Iyer spoke very little, mostly in monosyllables. Mallika turned away and thumbed through a photography magazine. Putting the phone down after the long conversation, Iyer lit up a cigarette.

'That was Preeti on the phone.'

'Oh. How is she?'

'Aren't you in touch? You two know each other from your schooldays, right?'

'Well, yes, but I haven't really seen her since the party at Ritu's house. But I guess you and Preeti must be quite close...'

'Yes. We are close friends. She confides in me and I lend her my shoulder sometimes. But there's nothing more than that.'

'Sorry... I didn't mean to pry.'

'I know. But I want you to know all the same. I'm not quite sure why.'

Iyer gazed at Mallika for a long time as he said this and stubbed out his cigarette in an ashtray. They ordered masala dosas from a restaurant on the ground floor of the building and relished it off the banana-leaf wrapping. The chutney was very spicy and Iyer happily polished off Mallika's share as well. Just as they rolled-up the wrappings, Mrs Hattangadi called to say that she was back at home and Iyer dropped Mallika back.

11

LAUGHTER AND TEARS

Mallika was about to leave the office one day when the telephone rang. Sriram had left already and she wondered who would phone so late in the day.

'Hello?'

'Mallika? Iyer here.' She was surprised to hear from him, as he was supposed to be out of Bombay on an assignment.

'When did you get back?'

'Today. Can we meet this evening?'

'No, I can't.'

'Found someone else while I was away?' Iyer teased her playfully.

'Oh, no such luck! I have to go to Ritu's house for a party. I had skipped the last one and it will look bad if I don't go again this time.'

Iyer laughed. 'Yeah, Shantanu has invited me as well. But once we go there, it will be difficult to get away soon.'

'I know, but I have no choice. Hey, what do you mean by "get away soon"?'

'Well, I am parked not far from your office actually. Why don't we go to my place for some time and go to the party later?'

'Your place?'

'Yes, there's something I want to...show you...' he said.

'Okay, fine, I'll meet you downstairs,' said Mallika, admitting, finally, to herself that the thought of meeting Iyer after nearly a whole week was exhilarating.

The early evening sky still flaunted a pinkish-orange glow as Mallika and Iyer reached his apartment.

'I wish we didn't have to go to that party.' Mallika said, stifling a yawn.

'Let me make some coffee first, I will be quick,' and Iyer dashed to the kitchen.

When he returned a few minutes later, Mallika had fallen asleep in a chair in what appeared to be a most uncomfortable posture. Iyer put the coffee mugs on a side table and watched her, his eyes taking in every line, every curve of the curled up figure, caressing each detail in his mind. He had missed her terribly while he was away. He felt protective of her and wished to be by her side always. Her face looked beautiful. His eyes rested leisurely on her curled eyelashes, usually hidden behind her glasses.

'What a baby,' Iyer whispered to himself.

He picked her up, surprised at her lightness, and moved towards the bedroom. Startled awake, Mallika tried getting off. To keep her from falling, Iyer held her closer for a moment before releasing her. Mallika touched her feet to the ground like a ballerina. They stood there motionless. Then his hands moved down her shoulders and held her by her elbows. Unwilling to part, he kissed her gently, affectionately, on the corner of her lips. Surprising herself, she kissed him back, more intimately than he had dared to; her hands, as if of their own will, going around him. Iyer held his hands back with a restraint that he had only just discovered he possessed, and finally raised his head to whisper, 'Look, either you say "stop" right now, this instant, or I shall not stop at anything.'

Mallika said nothing. She only whispered, 'I'm feeling so alive I could die at this moment and not regret it.'

When they woke up the next morning, they held hands, both waiting quietly for the other to utter the first word. It was around seven.

Soon Mallika broke the silence and asked, 'But what did you want to show me?'

To Mallika's great surprise, Iyer pulled out the bedside table drawer and brought out a thin gold ring with a tiny diamond and slipped it on to her finger. It fit snugly. Mallika smiled and embraced him. Looking engrossed in thought, she got out of bed saying, 'Let me make some tea.'

Iyer went to the restaurant downstairs to fetch some breakfast.

After they finished their tea and idlis, Mallika slipped the ring off, and returned it to him.

'I need to speak to my parents first. I will go home today itself.'

'Should I come with you? We can drive there.'

'No. I have to do this myself.'

Mallika's tone was serious and Iyer's voice quivered as he said, 'I'll wait. Call me as soon as you return?'

'Yes.'

Mallika took a bus that morning to go to Nashik, where her parents now lived. Before that, she made a quick phone call to Sriram to tell him she needed to go home for a couple of days.

She reached home a few hours later and immediately told her parents about Iyer. The questions began soon after.

'What did you say his name is?' Asked her father.

'David Iyer.'

'What sort of a name is that?'

'His mother was Jewish and his father Hindu. He is from Pondicherry.'

'So, he's half-Jew and half-Hindu?' her father stated the obvious, while pacing up and down the room, hands clasped behind his back.

'Yes.'

'Your mother tells me he saved your life.'

'He did.'

'You must thank him. Many, many thanks to him. I will meet him and thank him personally. But there's no reason to feel this kind of an obligation. Is that why you think you should marry him?'

'No.'

It was now her mother's turn to interrogate.

'Where does he work?'

'He is a photographer.'

'Is that a job? That is okay for a hobby. Is this why we educated you? You should have stayed at home instead of going to Bombay. We would have found a husband for you eventually. Girls your age are now married and mothers of one or two children. But look at you. Even now it is not too late. There is a nice boy that my aunt has suggested. He has a steady job with a bank and he will be a good match for you.'

All three fell silent for a moment before Mallika's mother splayed her hands helplessly.

'You tell her something,' she urged Mallika's father at last and trudged back into the kitchen.

Her father carried on with his own line of thought, as if the problem was purely technical.

'Had he been a Hindu, you could have married him, despite him being Tamilian and not Maharashtrian. Was his father a Brahmin?'

'I don't know, maybe. His father was a doctor. But their family was in the textile trade.'

'If his surname is Iyer, then his father must be Brahmin. Any Brahmin is acceptable for us. But this...this half-Jew and half-Hindu. Does he go to a temple or to a Jewish place of worship—what do they call it—a synagogue?'

'I don't know.'

'There are only a handful of Jews in India and you had to find one of them to marry?'

Mallika's mother had come back to the drawing room, the rolling pin in her hand.

'What does it matter if he prays or not? Which God will he pray to? And what will happen to your children if we let you marry him?'

A long pause followed as Mallika's parents exchanged panicky glances. Slowly sitting down in a chair, her mother asked Mallika in a calm voice, 'Has he touched you?'

Mallika did not answer. Tears brimmed in her eyes, and she wiped them with her dupatta.

Her mother stomped back to the kitchen and threw the rolling pin on the counter, slapping her forehead with her palm repeatedly, admonishing herself, 'karma, karma, karma maazha.'

Then she went back to rolling out the last few chapattis,

letting the round wooden board bang noisily against the counter.

Mallika ran to her room crying. She wished her brother were at home. He would have convinced her parents. Surely he would have. But he was away, studying in Australia. She wondered why she had thought her parents would agree and, in some way, help her make a decision. Without their consent, she was unable to make up her mind about marrying Iyer. But she had known even before she left Mumbai that they would not accept him. Why had she come home then? Was it just to reassure herself? Her doubts were not small enough to be ignored, but they were not definite enough to be shared with anyone, least of all with Iyer.

Back in Mumbai she did not have to say anything to Iyer. Just one look at her and he knew.

'They didn't agree, did they?'

'No. Maybe we should just give it more time for them to get used to the idea.'

'Yeah, let's do that. Maybe they will come around.'

He tried to appear cheerful but his face was sullen as they sat in silence, sipping coffee.

They continued to meet, less frequently than before. But the magic was gone.

It was just as well that the new assignment that Sriram had given Mallika kept her very busy, leaving her with very little time to think about Iyer.

12

THE FIRST ASSIGNMENT

Mallika had to urgently find an administrative assistant to replace her at Care People along with a new office in the suburbs, as the Nariman Point office was a temporary one provided by a generous friend of Dr Kasbekar's. Her other important assignment was to travel to villages in rural Maharashtra and visit at least three families who had suffered from the agrarian crisis.

'I don't really know where to start,' she began.

'It's natural, Mallika, if you feel a little out of depth at first. Don't dwell on that. You will just have to begin somewhere. I want you to lead this assignment.'

'Do you think it would be better if you came along as well?'

'No. I don't think we should both be doing the same thing. This will be an exploratory visit, so we can achieve more by dividing up and covering more ground. And you will learn more without me directing you.'

'Well, okay...'

'Here are some notes and clippings that I want you to read through,' he handed her a file folder as he continued with his instructions.

'You are to meet Mr Manoj Rathod in Wardha. He will give you information on where to go in the district. But before that, have you chosen volunteers to accompany you? We had discussed this earlier.'

'I have interviewed three so far. A few more will be coming in today. I will select two and keep the rest on standby for future work.'

'Good. At Wardha you should also visit the Agricultural Technology Centre set up by Dr Kabir Rehman.'

'Okay, Sriram.'

'I will be leaving for Yavatmal tomorrow morning. So... will you manage this?'

'Yes, I think so. I will prepare for the visit,' Mallika said faking a little confidence and returned to her desk to study the material Sriram had given her.

From her reading, she learned that Manoj Rathod was a middle-aged farmer in Wardha. He had immense knowledge and first-hand experience of the village economy. He was also the leader of a farmers' association in the Vidarbha region where he worked closely with the farming communities and spoke on their behalf at national meetings and international forums.

She also learnt that Dr Kabir Rehman was a respected agricultural scientist and an authority on rural development, having started a research and education foundation with centres that helped farmers across the country to access information on climate and monsoons, current crop prices and solutions for handling plant pests, diseases and fertilizers. Village children and youth flocked to the centres to acquire basic computer skills. In the evenings, both men and women farmers would gather at the same centres to discuss their problems. Through his research foundation, Dr Rehman hoped to improve agricultural production and apply scientific methods to solve the agrarian crisis in the country.

Mallika packed an old rucksack that once belonged to her brother. She and her volunteers were to take the twelve-hour overnight train, the Vidarbha Express, to Wardha Junction. The capacious Chhatrapati Shivaji Maharaj Terminus, or VT as it was commonly known, was crowded when Mallika arrived. She made slow progress to her platform, continually dodging passengers hurrying to their trains and coolies pushing trolleys loaded down with luggage. When she reached the platform it was empty; her train was yet to arrive. After walking about for a bit she found a vacant seat on a bench to sit and wait. A little boy walked to the edge of the platform, unzipped his trousers and let out a stream onto the track. Spotting him, a railway policeman approached, but the boy finished and quickly ran back to his parents who watched him indulgently through it all. An older woman sitting on the far side of the bench exchanged a disgusted look with Mallika. Soon the train rolled in and the platform burst into activity as the crowd waited to board. Eventually, Mallika climbed on and looked for her seat. She pushed her backpack onto the topmost berth and sat down next to the window.

As people poured onto the train, tramping up and down the aisles searching for their seats, she waited for the two volunteers to join her. The noise died down and departure time was imminent but they had not yet arrived. Other passengers settled into her compartment until just two seats remained empty. Then, almost without warning, the

train started and slowly moved out of the platform. Trying
not to panic, Mallika fanned herself with a newspaper and
wondered what to do next. Seconds later, her companions
arrived. Mallika greeted them as cheerfully as she could.
Taking in her expression, the young man smiled, 'You
thought we were not going to make it, huh?' and laughed as
he stowed their bags and plonked down in the seat opposite
her. Seema Gurav and Trevor Pinto were studying journalism
and wanted to use this assignment as part of a term project.
Seema settled down next to Mallika and twisted up her
long pony tail into a bun, dabbing her face and neck with
a handkerchief. A short while later she produced a package
of homemade rotis, potato bhaji and lemon pickle, enough
to feed all three of them.

'You know, Mallika, if there were fifteen of us, Seema
would still have brought enough to feed everyone,' Trevor
teased. 'For all our treks and picnics from college, Seema
is the caterer!'

'I can't help it!' laughed Seema. 'My mother is the one
who loves to feed my friends and now it's rubbed off on me.'

Following the delicious meal, they settled in their berths
to sleep. Mallika wondered what Iyer must be doing. She
hadn't met him in a long time. She had called him earlier
in the day to inform him about her trip to Wardha. But
the conversation had been short and she could sense that
Iyer was still hurting from their last meeting. The train was
dark except for the row of blue night lights glowing in the
corridor, one for each compartment. As her eyes fixed on
the one nearest to her, it flickered and dimmed, and then
popped out. She tried to prepare for her meeting with Manoj
Rathod and other families and soon drifted off to sleep.

In the morning, Mallika, Trevor and Seema waited in silence as their train neared Wardha Junction. It was 5:30 a.m. For a few minutes after getting off the train, they just waited there in a kind of huddle, rubbing their eyes and adjusting the bags on their shoulders before Mallika took charge.

'Let's get some tea first and then freshen up at the waiting rooms.'

They hired an autorickshaw to reach Manoj Rathod's house. The ground floor housed the office of the Indian Association of Farmers. As they introduced themselves to Mr Rathod, Mrs Rathod brought out plates of hot upma and a platter of cut half-ripe guavas sprinkled with salt and chilli powder. Trevor dug his spoon in the hot breakfast without waiting for the hosts to invite them to eat. The lady of the house began saying that hot water was ready for their baths when her husband cut in.

'No, no. Don't bother them about all that just now. They should head out to the village soon, morning hours are important if they want to meet people.'

Turning to the little group, he urged them to finish breakfast and continued talking.

'I have spoken to some of the villagers already. You should speak first to Vikram Sonare, a young man who works at the institute. He will take you around to meet people. He will also show you the institute. Then you can come back here and, please, have your lunch with us.'

Finally, Mallika got a chance to speak.

'We would like to talk to you as well about the Association of Farmers and your work.'

'We will have plenty of time in the evening for that.

Right now, you should go to Sonsawali. Sorry for rushing you like this, but most of the villagers will go to the fields and you won't be able to meet anyone if you are late.'

'Yes, we understand. We will leave immediately. Can we hire an autorickshaw to take us there?'

'I have called one auto driver, Parshuram. I know him well and he will take you everywhere and bring you back here.'

Parshuram made ample use of the horn. Mallika, Trevor and Seema sat close together in the autorickshaw, taking in Wardha town as it slowly woke up. Most shop shutters were down and traffic minimal as they drove through the town centre. Eventually, they hit the highway. After about twenty minutes of breezing past green fields, they turned left into a narrow road. It was rough and Parshuram manouvered the vehicle in a zig-zag style to avoid the nasty potholes, jostling his passengers from side to side. But he ignored the smaller potholes, going right through them and tossing the three of them up and down. Soon they reached a dirt road edged by more fields of tall golden grass. A village hamlet came into view just ahead and they stopped in an open space. As they stepped out, Mallika noticed a large peepal tree. In the shade, a group of men sat on the platform around the tree trunk. Two of the younger men stood up on seeing the visitors. One came forward briskly and spoke to Parshuram. Mallika asked him if he knew where Vikram Sonare lived. He nodded towards the houses in the village and led them in that direction.

Both sides of the narrow lane were lined with short brick houses and one could touch the edge of their clay-tiled roofs by just stretching out a hand. Mallika noticed Trevor doing just that. The outer walls of the houses were painted white, blue or yellow, though some stood out, unpainted and grey. A few houses had thatched roofs and mud walls. First turning right and then left in the narrow lane, they reached a small clearing surrounded by four houses. One house had a well outside and an ox tied to a stubby pole. A boy of about four looked up at them startled. Wiping his runny nose on his sleeve, he ran inside the hut. His navy blue shorts were covered with patches of mud from sitting on the ground. In the next instant, a thin young man appeared from inside the hut. He wore black trousers and a white vest. Taking water from a bucket near the well, he washed his face and quickly wiped it on a much-worn towel hanging over his left shoulder.

'Rathod saheb had said you would be coming today,' smiled Vikram Sonare, coming straight to the point. An older woman came out of the house, adjusting her pallu to cover her bushy grey hair. Her face was darkened from years of working in the sun. Four tiny blue dots were tattooed in a floral pattern on her forehead. Kashibai Sonare invited them in. Vikram spread out a plastic woven mat on the floor for the guests while he stood against the wall. Kashibai sat with her back to the wall in what seemed to be her usual place. The hut was about eight feet wide and twelve feet long. Halfway across the length of the house was a two-feet high mud wall that partially separated the outer room from the kitchen. Vikram's brother Vishwas and his wife Surekha emerged out of the far end of the hut, which was the kitchen. They all sat cross-legged, arranging themselves in a semi-circle on the mat. A thin rope fixed at the doorway ran along one wall with clothes piled over it on one end.

On the other side, stood a wood fire, stoking beneath a blackened aluminium pot bubbling with rice and water. The smoke from the fire stung their eyes and the steam from the boiling rice spread a damp aroma in the windowless house.

Apart from the firelight and the daylight streaming in from the doorway, it was quite dark. Surekha sat in the space that led to the small kitchen, with a baby in her lap. She had covered her shoulders completely with her red sari. Her hair was tied with a white rubber band into a short ponytail. She smiled at the girls and offered to make tea for everyone. They all thanked and declined. The small boy they had seen earlier emerged from the kitchen. He had finished his meal and stepped outside to wash his hands. He ran inside and picked up his schoolbag from behind Mallika, who noticed his very large brown eyes staring at her curiously.

For a while they all sat in silence. Until Kashibai began to speak.

'One evening seven months ago, my husband returned home from a visit to the bank. He had been refused a loan for the second time. We had no money left even for daily expenses. Despite that, I told him it was alright. We would all try to find work and earn daily wages as we often do and live our life the way we could. But he was very upset that day. The next morning, he was missing from the house. I found him lying in the cowshed behind the house. He had consumed pesticide and killed himself.'

There was silence again for a while, accompanied by the sounds of crackling fire and the put-put of bubbling rice.

'I don't cry now. What is the use of crying? If nobody wants to help us we can only help ourselves and live the

life that comes to us every morning. Every morning—I have
told my sons and daughter-in-law this—every morning we
live the life that comes to us and go to sleep with it. I am
living now for my children and my grandchildren. Whatever
I do is for them. They are my life now and all my work is
for them.

'Two months ago, the government brought cows and
offered them as a relief for our pathetic situation. Now tell
me...the people in the government, I think, are educated and
know some basic things before they make such decisions. Do
they not know that to keep a cow, one requires fodder and
water? Do they not know that there is shortage of fodder
and water in this region? What are we going to do with the
cow? It only gives us four litres of milk, which does not come
to much money. And should I starve my family and feed
the cow? And the cow was not free. It was only subsidized.
I had to pay Rs 5,000 for it and Rs 500 as commission to
the officer who was looking after this whole work.'

Vishwas began talking as his mother fell silent.

'I tell my mother that I will take the cow and leave it
at the collector's house and tell him to raise it. I have told
others in the village also to do this. If they also listen to
the suggestion, the collector will have a nice herd of cows
in his front yard.'

Mallika asked Vishwas, 'So, for how long do you work
in the fields?'

'All day. Now by nine, nine-thirty we will leave for the
fields, all three of us. Even my mother works, at her age.
She is nearly sixty but she still works. We walk for one hour
to reach the fields. We eat in the afternoon, our only meal
for the day. We have only one meal every day. We cannot

afford to eat more. Eating less means we can stay awake and not become lazy or sleepy. We return home by six in the evening or sometimes seven and then go to sleep.'

It was time to move on from the Sonare household. Exchanging namastes with the family, they left. Mallika held hands with Surekha. Sharing a moment with the young mother was the only thing she could do then, feeling helpless as she did at the family's situation and struggles, and yet Surekha seemed to reassure her with her smile. There was still hope, her eyes seemed to say, and the baby on her arm bobbed his head, smiling in agreement.

The next house belonged to an old couple, the Madhes. Their only son had hung himself to death three months ago. Their daughter-in-law looked on in silence. Her teenage son was the man of the house now. Vikram, who was maybe just a little bit older, stood next to him and held his shoulder for a moment. Mallika asked the boy a few questions. But he remained silent. I don't know what will happen to us, the boy's silence seemed to convey. Fear and responsibility had prematurely aged him.

As they walked back to their vehicle, Vikram said, 'That boy, Chandar, is younger than me but he is a friend. I can understand what he is going through. When my father committed suicide, I know how I felt even though I have an elder brother. Chandar doesn't even have a brother. So I keep an eye on him and meet him almost everyday.'

'Does he confide in you, Vikram?' asked Mallika.

'Yes, sometimes.'

'What does he say?'

'Mostly that he feels like running away from this world.'

From the village, the group drove on to the institute.

Vikram Sonare sat in the front seat with Parshuram. A narrow lane lined with small white houses on either side ended in front of a larger house painted blue. INSTITUTE OF AGRICULTURAL TECHNOLOGY, WARDHA, read the signboard, FOUNDED BY DR KABIR AHMED, ESTD 1998. The door was open and as they entered, a man rose from behind a desk and came forward as Vikram introduced him.

'Meet Mr Pramod Ghosh. He has taught me everything that I know so far about the institute and also about using a computer.'

The short, bespectacled man smiled and ran his fingers along his bushy moustache.

'So pleased to meet you. Rathodji had said that you would be visiting and that I should show you around the institute.'

He spread out his arms indicating the large hall. On one wall there was a blackboard listing jowar, bajra, cotton, soyabean, orange and groundnuts in chalk. The first two crops had tick marks against them.

'We discuss cropping patterns with the farmers,' explained Mr Ghosh.

'Over the years, cotton has been grown here. The cost for the seeds, fertilizers and pesticides is high. We want to begin cultivating jowar and bajra so that there is a ready source of foodgrains and fodder for the cattle. This institute also provides weather information to help the farmers decide when it is best to sow. Until Dr Ahmed opened this centre and others like it, the only sources of information for the farmers were the traders, who were not really that knowledgeable, and other farmers like themselves. It is only recently that the farmers started coming to get help from the centres. We try to explain the science behind the routine that the farmers follow in cultivation. Now agriculture experts sometimes visit us and share their research findings with the farmers to improve their yields and advise them on cultivation problems. We also teach the use of computers to some of the schoolchildren and others. Vikram here is our computer operator, but he does more than that. I do some of the teaching, but he leads most of the practical sessions and explains how it all works, in words the learners can understand better.'

A rush of tinkles brought in Rupali, who was startled to see all of them. Mr Ghosh continued unperturbed, 'This is Rupali Parab. She is the daughter of our sarpanch. She is learning how to operate a computer from Vikram. And...I think I just revealed a secret.' The last bit caught Vikram off guard to everyone's amusement. He signalled to her to stay.

When they left, Mr Ghosh joined Mallika and the others for a part of the journey back. Trevor offered him his seat while he shared the driver's seat with Parshuram.

They were silent until they reached Manoj Rathod's home. Mr Rathod was out. After a quick lunch, they retired for a while to a room on the ground floor where three mattresses and bed linen lay waiting for them. Seema was the first to speak.

'I think Kashibai and her daughter-in-law, Surekha, are taking the situation better than the elder son, Vishwas.'

'You are right. I guess men seem to lose hope faster than women,' agreed Trevor.

Mallika stopped leafing through the notes that she had made during the visits to the two families and said, 'There is also the issue of "losing face" where the menfolk are concerned. They look upon themselves as the earners and providers and when they cannot fulfil their roles, they take their own lives. It's very tragic. The women go on, living and working for their children and themselves. They channel their grief into hard work. I dread to think what will happen to the teenage boy in the second family we visited, the Madhe family. Did you see his expression?'

Trevor nodded, 'Yeah, it was pure fear. He must be feeling cornered now, having to take care of his mother and grandparents. The loss of his father must be on his mind constantly. What Vikram told us only affirms this.'

'And his mother,' added Seema, 'did you notice she was in the house physically, but lost somewhere? Her eyes looked dead. I kept looking at her off and on, but she just didn't seem to be there.'

'You are either very brave Seema or very innocent. I didn't dare take a second glance at her. We'll talk with Mr Rathod in the evening. Let's get some rest now.'

They were rolling out the mattresses to prepare for a nap when Mrs Rathod brought in a jug of water and drinking glasses, telling them to come back upstairs for tea at about four.

It was dark outside when Mallika, Seema and Trevor, still groggy from their nap, trudged wearily back upstairs. Feeling guilty about their late reappearance, Mallika apologized to Mrs Rathod, 'I'm sorry we didn't come up earlier for tea. I think we slept too long.'

'It is okay. You had the train journey last night and walked so much this morning. So I knew you all must be really tired.' Mallika followed Mrs Rathod into the kitchen where, without a word, her hostess handed her a stack of stainless steel plates. Mallika set them along the long, narrow dining table, while Seema helped carry in the food. Mr Rathod took his seat at one end and the rest sat on either side of him. Without preamble, Mrs Rathod placed two rotis on each plate and everyone helped themselves to dal, a spinach curry and a dry vegetable dish of karela and aloo. A platter of sliced onions, tomatoes and cucumber was passed around. Mrs Rathod joined them halfway through the meal. They finished it off with some rice and dal and small bowls of buttermilk. Then Mrs Rathod served everyone a square piece of gul-papdi. Quickly polishing off his share of the wheat flour and jaggery sweet, Trevor looked longingly at the closed box next to Mrs Rathod. Seema glared at him. When Mrs Rathod picked up a sweet for herself, her husband went to wash his hands. The others followed while Mallika waited for their hostess to finish her meal.

'The dinner was delicious, maushi,' said Seema, returning to the table.

'Yes, aunty, it was very nice,' added Trevor.

Mallika then told Mr Rathod about their visit to Sonsawali and the Agricultural Technology Centre.

'Yes,' said Mr Rathod. 'It is no longer possible for farmers to make a living from farming alone. The technology centre will help them increase their production and maybe earn a little more than they do now.'

Mallika nodded in agreement, adding, 'And the rains being unpredictable every year must also be affecting crop production.'

'Yes, Mallika, you are correct. But delayed rains and drought are not the only causes of hardship for farmers.

Other things are far more destructive to their already hard lives.'

He looked at Mallika and then turned to the others, challenging them with his piercing gaze. Trevor broke the pause, 'What can do more harm than the lack of rains?'

Mr Rathod retorted, 'The policies set by our government and international trade bodies. They are projected as policies to help farmers but actually they accomplish just the reverse. The cost of growing crops and the prices of seeds, fertilizers and pesticides have gone up many times over. But the income the farmer receives for his crop has not increased as much. In the language of so-called economists, the input costs are much higher than the income from farming!'

'But I have heard that the government allocates funds for agriculture every year. Doesn't that help the farmers?' Seema shot back.

Mr Rathod laughed, showing his big white teeth, 'Very good, so you know that the government is doing at least something for farmers! But do you know what the problem is? The policy for agriculture and allocation of funds is decided at the centre, whereas the implementation...'

'The implementation is a state-level responsibility?' asked Mallika.

'Haan...ekdum barabar kaha aapne. My young friends, can you see how it is for the farmers? The way the government at the centre and state levels keep fighting with each other and accusing each other, the farmers are the worst sufferers...they are waiting not only for the monsoon but for action from the government that will help them when they need it the most.'

'But don't the farmers also get subsidies from the government?' asked Seema.

'Yes, they do, but not enough. People like you think that farmers get many subsidies—water, electricity, loan waivers. But very few know the reality of it. Just compare the amounts spent by the government on agriculture and subsidies for farmers with what the government gives to other industries and businesses. You will realize how badly farmers are treated. They always get a raw deal.'

'But other industries and businesses make money and pay taxes, don't they?' Trevor interrupted.

'Yes, they definitely do. The farmers are generating money, too. When we get bumper crops and export them, the nation makes money. That adds to the GDP, the gross domestic product. But more importantly, aren't farmers providing food to the nation? Is that any less important than generating money?'

'Not everything can be compared in monetary terms,' agreed Mallika.

'A large portion of our population is engaged in agriculture and other related occupations. Can you imagine what would happen if all these farmers and labourers gave up agriculture? Who would grow food for us? We already have unemployment problems. Think how many people would flood the job market if more and more farmers quit agriculture? They are already doing it, especially the younger generation. No one wants to become a farmer now,' said Mr Rathod.

A thoughtful silence ensued.

Noticing the time, Mallika decided to wind up the conversation. 'We have asked Parshuram to come early tomorrow. We will be spending the entire day out in the villages and will go directly to Wardha station afterwards to catch the train.'

'That is a good plan. I hope you have found what you came here for.'

'Yes, it has been a great learning experience.'

'I may not see you tomorrow morning as I will be going to Nagpur very early. Do give my regards to Dr Sriram. I hope to meet him, too, sometime.'

'Yes, thank you so much for everything.'

'No problem, no problem,' Mrs Rathod joined in, beaming at them. 'We enjoyed having you here.' She held a small packet of sweets that she handed over to Seema while smiling at Trevor with a twinkle in her eye and said, 'It's some gul-papdi for the train journey.'

Trevor blushed and grabbed the packet from Seema.

13

TIME OF DEBT

In Yavatmal, Sriram met Devdutt Hande at a lodging house. The burly reporter worked for a newspaper in Nagpur and spent several days every month in villages throughout Vidarbha. His once wheatish skin had by now tanned to a dark shade of mahogany. His hair, raggedy from regular exposure to the sun, dust and grime, was speckled with grey strands that stood out in the ample black.

Putting down the cup of tea that he had finished drinking in three gulps, he fixed Sriram with a steady gaze.

'I spend anywhere from five to twenty days here every month. Not all of the areas are accessible by public transport, so I ride my motorcycle, or sometimes even a bicycle, from village to village. I speak to the farmers, the village, the taluka and district officials. And also to the women and children. They are really going through some very tough times. Do you know that an average of three farmers commit suicide in these districts everyday? That's one every eight hours. They are unable to repay their debts and frustrated by a vicious situation, swallowing pesticide is the only way to escape a dreadful life. You can imagine how much worse it is for the widows, the old parents and children of these farmers. Their troubles are doubled and trebled.'

He looked pointedly at Sriram, who was finding it hard to drink the over-sweetened tea.

'Anyway, what is your interest here? You mentioned something on the phone but I'm not sure exactly what it is you want.'

'I am in the process of setting up a new division of Care People to focus on the rural areas.'

'An NGO?'

'Yes.'

Sriram noticed the scepticism on Devdutt's face but ignored it.

'You are not the first one. Many NGO people have already come here. So many of them come to undertake studies and then prepare reports. Some of them come for three days, some of them spend just half a day in one village and go back and write voluminous reports. What do you want to do? Write another report?'

Sriram paused and finished drinking his tea before speaking.

'I am here to spend some time talking to these people in order to understand their situation. I am a doctor by profession and would like to try counselling some of the people here. Not just counsel individual farmers but form a people's support network. I can also conduct group counselling where they can share their problems with each other and cooperate to find solutions.'

Sriram felt that he had caught the reporter's attention. Their drained teacups sat on matching chipped saucers. Devdutt leaned back in silence, and lit a cigarette.

'Counselling is just one thing. I would like our work to go beyond that. Think of it as an all-round rural infrastructure project,' added Sriram.

Devdutt took a long puff from his cigarette and asked, 'What exactly would you be doing?'

'There are certain things that people like me and millions of others living in the cities—I mean urban citizens—take for granted. That is, the urban infrastructure. Right from birth to death, a person living in a city has access to everything— food, water, home, schools, college, entertainment, and of course basic necessities like electricity, roads, shops in which to buy goods and everything that anyone requires. But can we say the same for our rural areas?'

'But that has been the case for years and years. There's nothing new in what you are saying.'

'Exactly. That just proves how critical it is now for us to finally define basic rural infrastructure. Things that must be available in all parts of our vast country wherever there is human habitation. Then find out if anything is being done for making the infrastructure available or whether it has been addressed at all, or if it is supposed to be done but is not being done, like scores of other things.'

'Isn't that a huge proposition? How much do you expect to do?'

'I want to begin in a small way somewhere, assess the most basic needs of infrastructure and see where we are. Then try to push for policy and legislation eventually to get these things done. I'm sure these issues have been addressed in the five-year plans but much of it must have got left out and even much more not implemented.'

'Well, Dr Kasbekar, where do you actually want to start?'

'Please, call me Sriram. I think we should meet the panchayat members and then some of the families in this village. If you could introduce me to some of them it would be helpful.'

'Sure, sure. I have been working in these areas for the past four years now. I know a fairly good number of people and I can put you in touch with some of them.'

As they walked through Kasola village, they met Dhanaji Pawar, who was about sixty years old. When Sriram and Devdutt entered his house, Dhanaji asked them to sit and then began talking as if he had been waiting for this very conversation.

'I would have offered you something to eat but there is nothing left now.'

He opened the two brass dabbas and showed them the empty insides.

'I can sell these two dabbas and might get some money for them but they are from the old days when my wife and I got married, so I am keeping them for as long as I can. I was walking near the grain shop yesterday and found some red chillies that had fallen on the ground near the entrance. I snatched them up before anyone saw me and brought them home and ate them. I had to drink four glasses of water as the chillies were really hot. But that was good as it quenched my hunger, at least for a while. This is how it is everyday. We have sold most of our land and all of the gold jewellery that belonged to my wife and my daughter-in-law. My son died two months ago. He ate rat poison. My wife died some days after that. She couldn't bear the trauma. My daughter-in-law has gone to the next village. She is a wage worker on a farm there. She has taken her

two children, so that they can also work with her. I cannot
work as my knees ache and my arms have no strength. I
could try to till the land—whatever is left—but I have no
money for buying seeds. Only after my daughter-in-law
gets some money that she can spare can I do that. Till that
happens, I will just have to wait.'

After spending an hour of silent consolation with
Dhanaji Pawar, Sriram and Devdutt walked on and met
the widow of a farmer who had set a big bundle of hay on
fire and jumped into it, ending his life. The woman joined
her hands in namaste when Sriram greeted her. But there
was no change in her expression as she continued to sit at
the entrance of her hut. She said nothing and stared into
nothingness. Sriram had no choice but to leave her alone
and walk away.

Later that evening, Sriram said goodbye to Devdutt
Hande who had to move on elsewhere for his work. They
agreed to keep in touch.

Instead of returning directly to Bombay, Sriram decided
to go to another village in the Yavatmal district, travelling by
state transport. At the stop, an ST bus arrived and without
thinking he boarded it, curious to see where it would take
him. Three hours later, he got off at the last stop with a
few other people. It was early evening. He walked for what
seemed like many hours along a dusty road. Suddenly, a
group of houses appeared and he entered the village of
Raveri, as a dusty yellow signboard proclaimed. The village
seemed desolate until he chanced upon Dhondiba, who was
sitting alone on a culvert. His dhoti was soiled. His dusty
turban had once been a fiery red. The shirt he wore had
seen much better days. On a closer look, one could see the

efforts at re-stitching the buttons and several darned patches repaired by loving hands. Dhondiba sat listlessly staring into space, watching some birds in the far off trees. Sriram made some effort to talk to him. But it was almost as if he was not aware of Sriram. After introducing himself, he asked the man what he was thinking.

'Do you have a bidi?'

'No.' Sriram wished he had carried bidis for moments such as this. But Dhondiba did not seem to mind much. Once he finally began to talk, Sriram listened without interrupting him.

'It wasn't always like this. Our village was full of people and bustling with activity at one time. The fields were lush. Crops danced in the evening breeze and the granary was full. After selling some grain, each house in the village had enough to feed their family, and even for any unexpected relatives visiting. But now things have changed. First, we stopped growing as much of the food grains. Cotton, we grew cotton instead. It was like white gold. It brought prosperity. I ask you, does anything last forever? No. So the cotton caught blight and disease. We needed more pesticides. We needed to buy new seeds, hybrid seeds, then more pesticides. The expenses grew. We took loans from the banks. Then the price of cotton fell. Our savings shrank. So we took more loans from banks. When the banks did not give, we turned to the village moneylender. Money was easy to get. Difficult to return at first, and then, impossible. The interest grew faster than the cotton. Everything else was shrinking: our land, as we sold off some to pay the debt; our self-respect, as the burden of the debt grew we lost face among our loved ones and community. Which self-respecting man would like to say he can't support his family or continue in his profession? There was no help from the sarkari log. First the government turned their back on us. Then it was God or nature, whatever you want to call it. There were no rains and the cotton shrank even further and the debts kept growing. Why wouldn't they? They were not crops. Men fought to keep the debts from growing but all in vain. After a man is finished with fighting, there is only one way out. Death! Several men chose it, calling out to "Death" with a noose or a bottle of pesticide as temptation. And it came willingly. Like an eager bride. Death is an eager bride when you are a farmer in debt.'

Dhondiba laughed loudly. Shaking and displaying open gums and missing teeth.

Sriram waited patiently, knowing that his companion's sudden laughter was a preamble to something profound.

'I am a farmer and I have no food to eat. Can there be anything funnier than this?'

Dhondiba laughed again until his eyes became moist.

'If the hunger becomes unbearable, I drink water. That gives the feeling of being full, at least for sometime. On some days there is only water to be had.

'Two weeks ago, Ramdas Kardilay, a farmer just like me, hanged himself. Villagers out in the early morning hours to relieve themselves in the open fields saw his body hanging from a tree in the distance. The whole village came running to the tree on hearing the news. His wife and three daughters are left now to deal with life.'

Dhondiba fell silent for a moment, then let out a sigh.

'Weddings are good. On those days, I can have a full meal for three days in a row. But there has been no wedding in my village for a very long time now.'

He looked into the horizon at the birds and fell silent again. As if he was alone.

Sriram stood up, put his hand on the man's shoulder and then walked away. He wanted to find the family of the farmer who had died two weeks ago, to talk to his wife and three daughters. But how does a man face a woman whose husband, after years of working hard to make ends meet, has killed himself? What would be her sense of despair to know that she must now bring up their three daughters all by herself? He kept walking. He did not seek out the woman with three daughters.

Sriram walked past the end of the village and carried on along the dusty road till it met another narrow lane that took him to the highway. He continued walking towards a bus stop that he had spotted in the distance. About five or six people were already waiting, a few of them sitting on the ground, some standing. Sriram could not decide whether to take a bus and return home or stay for another day. He walked a little further and reached a petrol pump. A small, single-storey building stood next to it. A thin wooden board hung loose from a solitary nail. The board read 'Shriram Lodge'. Laughing aloud at the coincidence, Sriram went inside and booked a room. That night, lying awake on his bed, he made a plan. He would need to recruit more volunteers to carry out his vision: students as primary data collectors, and an experienced statistician to analyze the data and write reports.

Sriram knew there were no instant solutions to the crisis affecting such large parts of rural Maharashtra. But he also knew that he could start in a small way through mass contact with the villagers. If they could gather sufficient relevant information, it could perhaps be used to help them, though he did not immediately know how exactly. Perhaps it would be good to walk all the way through the villages. Yes, it might be best to do that. Maybe they could undertake a padayatra—a walk through the villages of Maharashtra. It would take at least a month to complete such a walk or maybe longer. They must plan well to keep it to a month. Anything longer might be unmanageable. Three or four people might be required to make an initial exploratory study, before they could finalize the plan for such a large scale walk.

The surge of ideas made him restless. He switched on the light. He took out the various district maps of Maharashtra, on which he had made several pencil markings, and a stapled set of papers, on which the villages in each district were listed. Sriram thought about what route they could take and reviewed the list of villages, ticking off a few listed under different districts. Picking up his cellphone, he called Mallika. But it was out of coverage area and he gave up after a few attempts. Then he remembered that she was in Wardha anyway. They were not too far from each other, less than forty miles. But he would have to wait till they both were back in Mumbai.

14

BHASKAR PRABHU

The next morning Mallika, Seema and Trevor zipped out
again in Parshuram's auto. Vikram Sonare joined them on
the highway, shouting 'Good morning' over the tuk-tuk's
rattle as he got in.

They stopped at Kosurla, a village of about 800 people.
A few men and two women milled about at the edge of a
large hole, looking down into it. Mallika and her group
drew closer and saw a man digging a well. He had been
digging for seven days, they learned, stopping only to sleep.
No water had appeared so far but he was determined to
keep digging until he either struck water or died. Everyday
his wife threw down food to him in a plastic bag, but he
hadn't eaten anything for the last two days. Another man in
khaki pants and a navy-blue shirt crouched on the ground,
snapping away urgently with his camera.

He called gently to the digger, 'Do exactly what you
are doing. Don't change anything just because I am taking
pictures.' The man in the hole continued his work without
a word. After so many days, he had developed a rhythm
to his digging: he heaved the pickaxe over his head before

letting it fall to the ground as if controlled by an invisible spring. The chiselled end rang twice on the hard ground, and then, the axe flew back up in an arc once more.

The photographer climbed down into the hole, speaking to the digger while taking more close-up shots. When he straightened up, he noticed Mallika, Seema and Trevor looking down at him. One of the villagers threw down a rope and as he grabbed it to hoist himself back up, his camera dangling from around his neck, Trevor recognized him and whispered to Mallika.

'That's Bhaskar Prabhu, the reporter and deputy editor of *The Nation's Voice*. He also heads the new photo magazine *Rural India*.'

Mallika immediately started a conversation with the well-known journalist.

'Hello, Bhaskar sir. We are volunteers with Care People from Mumbai. We've been here for the past two days to meet the villagers.'

He grimaced slightly and cleaned the dust from his shirt. 'What have you done during your time here?' he asked while making adjustments to his camera.

Mallika hesitated a little.

'We...we went to Sonsawali village yesterday and met with two families there. We talked to them, the Sonare and the Madhe family. Vikram Sonare is also with us today. He showed us the Institute of Agriculture Technology.'

At the mention of Sonare, he looked up from his camera, and turning to Vikram said, 'I hope all is well with your mother and the rest of your family.'

'Yes, Bhaskar saheb, sab theek hai. When are you coming home again?'

'Soon, I will come again soon.' Turning to the rest he asked, 'And what have you learned so far?'

'We...we found out about the daily routine the farmers follow. The kind of hardships they face that people like us can never imagine. They seem not to exist for people like us, living our protected and comfortable city lives.'

'Why do you think that is?' he stared at Mallika and waited for her to answer.

Feeling a little taken aback, Mallika paused to think and then continued.

'What we understood from our observations, and also from talking to Mr Manoj Rathod, is that they spend more money to grow the crops but do not earn enough in return. That seems to be one of the main problems. They are also burdened with debt that they cannot repay.'

'You seem to have found out what is happening. But do you know why this is happening? Or how it all started?'

'Well, we have just begun our research. But we hope to learn from you. Would you be willing to let us accompany you, sir?'

'Do any of you speak Marathi? I know that Vikram does.'

'Yes, we all do,' they chorused.

'Sir, I'm Mallika Joshi and I am in charge of our small group. My colleagues are Trevor Pinto and Seema Gurav.'

'I am Bhaskar Prabhu.'

Trevor spoke up animatedly as he came forward, 'Yes sir, we know. I have attended one of your lectures.'

'Is that so? Which one?'

'Sir, last year at the Institute of Social Sciences, in Bombay.'

Bhaskar smiled and then turned back into his serious self.

'Well, you can join me. I want you to ask questions in Marathi and translate for me when required. I can understand a bit of Marathi but cannot speak it. I will be speaking in Hindi.'

'Sir, Seema and I are studying journalism at the University of Mumbai and I would like to work for you sir, for your magazine, *Rural India*.'

Smiling, he replied, 'Well, we will see about that another time. Right now, I am going to meet this family of two brothers. A young colleague who speaks Marathi was supposed to be with me, but at the last minute his plans changed. So you've come along at the right time.'

After reaching the family's home, they sat outside on a cot made of rope and bamboo. Two women sat across from them. Their children, two boys and three girls, sat or stood nearby. Sita, the older woman, had lost her husband six months ago. He had swallowed rat poison. Savitri's husband had died three months ago after drinking pesticide. The two men were brothers.

Bhaskar sat in tense silence, trying to think of something appropriate to say to these two women who now shared the same house, the same tragedy. Mallika, Trevor and Seema looked on in a hushed silence. Bhaskar spoke gently. The words came to him with increasing difficulty every time he repeated them to so many such families over the years: 'I am sorry to hear about your loss.'

He looked at the elder and then the younger sister-in-law. Sita covered her head and mouth with her sari's edge. Her empty eyes must have once shone with zest. A sari draped Savitri's shoulders but her uncovered head revealed premature grey strands. Her eyes held a different look, smouldering with anger. Neither of the women replied; there was only a silent acceptance of the condolences. A young girl of about three peeped out from behind Savitri, the spitting image of her mother. Her searching eyes took in the new visitors, too innocent to understand where her father and uncle had vanished suddenly. Bhaskar Prabhu took out his exercise book and a form. 'I want to ask some questions related to your farming. Is that okay?'

Savitri turned to look at him directly and inclined her head in agreement.

'How much land do you have?'

'Five acres.'

'How much of it is under cultivation?'

'Three.'

'How much do you invest per acre for a crop?'

'Twenty thousand rupees.'

As she translated Bhaskar Prabhu's questions into Marathi, Mallika remembered her own enquiries with the Madhe and Sonare families and realized their inadequacy.

Were the seeds changed? Where did they sell the produce? What price did they get? Had they incurred a loan? Which bank did they receive the loan from? Did they borrow from a private money lender? What was the amount of each loan? What was the interest rate charged by the bank? How much did the moneylender charge?

For each question, Savitri's answers revealed an increasingly dire situation. Her rage seemed to ascend as she answered each question.

It was almost an hour before they bid goodbye to the family. Mallika had two packets of biscuits, which she offered to the children. They looked up at Savitri for permission, which she granted with a slight nod. They ran to Mallika and took the biscuits with a great deal of joy.

As they left, Mallika blurted out to Bhaskar, 'Your questions were so comprehensive. I barely asked the people *we* met anything.'

'So where are you going next?'

'In the evening we return to Mumbai. We may return to Vidarbha again for a longer visit. But...where else would you suggest we go?'

'Perhaps some of the poorest districts in other states. Maybe you should spend some time there. Live there, if possible.'

'Other states...you mean like Andhra, Orissa, West Bengal? Which districts?' asked Vikram

'Mehboob Nagar, Vijayanagaram in Andhra; Kalahandi, Nuapada, Koraput in Orissa; Purulia in West Bengal.'

'What about Bihar, Rajasthan and Uttar Pradesh?'

'Barmer, Ganga Nagar in Rajasthan; Banda Basti in UP; Purnia in Bihar.' Vikram was scribbling all the names in a small notebook.

'Can we...can I meet you sometime in Mumbai?' asked Mallika.

'I am on the move constantly. But yes, we can try and meet. Send me an email.'

Mallika still had too many questions to ask as Prabhu got into his car and drove off to his next destination while she and the others proceeded to Wardha station.

As the auto sped down the road, Vikram Sonare turned around from his front seat to discuss some of his ideas. After several increasingly louder repetitions, they finally heard what he was saying above the din of the three-wheeler.

'I have a burning desire to bring change into our lives in the village. I want to use technology and connect with other people like me throughout India.'

At the station they had to wait for an hour as the train was delayed, and Vikram knew he had to speak up now and share his thoughts with his new friends.

'In 1857, people were able to rise together in a revolt against the East India Company. That was more than a hundred and fifty years ago. Even in those times, they were able to communicate and come together, and they shook not just the company but the British Empire as well. We all know what happened after that.'

'Yes, but what's your point, Vikram?' asked Trevor.

'Today, I know there are so many people who think like me. I want to bring them all together.'

Mallika was intrigued and asked, 'Think like you, what do you mean?'

'I mean that they want better lives than the constant hand-to-mouth existence. And if that is not happening because of the people who rule the country and make all decisions on our behalf, then we need to force them to listen to us. We need to shake them up, like our ancestors did so many years ago. But first, we need to bring them all together, build a network so that everyone is connected and instant communication is easy.'

'Vikram, what are the one or two things that you would say have affected the course of agriculture, especially in Vidarbha? I ask you because you live here, you're from a farming family and you have seen things from up close all your life,' asked Mallika.

'Traditionally, Mallika, the farmers in Vidarbha and

other regions of Maharashtra like Marathwada grew hardy traditional varieties of cotton that required little water and were also pest resistant. The government procured it from these farmers for the cotton federation. This was a monopoly. There were traders who bought the cotton on behalf of the federation. So a portion of what the federation paid went into the pockets of traders. If the prices offered were good, the traders benefited much more than the farmers. The farmers had an assured buyer for decades. But then, in the nineties came the economic liberalization. The government withdrew the monopoly procurement schemes. The farmers were left at the mercy of private traders and their reduced prices.

'Added to all this was the unknown evil boon of Bt Cotton. A genetically modified variety of cotton that was resistant to boll-worm infestation but susceptible to sucking pests. To buy a packet of seeds for this new variety, the farmer paid thrice the amount he would pay for a packet of non-Bt variety. There was additional cost for fertilizers and pesticides. But the new variety promised high yield. The government at the state level promised to pay Rs 2,700 per quintal of cotton during election campaigns and after getting elected, they brought down the price to Rs 1,700. The advance bonus of Rs 500 per quintal was also withdrawn. Then the rains failed, reducing the cotton yield and adding to their burden. What were the farmers to do? Several of them consumed pesticide, seeing it as the only way out of their misery. My father too. But the government didn't accept that the price reduction triggered the suicides. It was like saying we have done what we wanted, now if you want to do this, well, we will let you die if you have to. We are not responsible for it.'

There was a chilling silence, that broke only when the train hooted to signal its departure.

Mallika shook his hand and said to Vikram, 'Come to Mumbai. We have to continue this conversation. I'm sorry we are going away just as you started to tell us about your ideas.' They promised to exchange emails as they parted. Trevor gave Vikram a quick bear hug before hopping onto the moving train.

'I will come, I will come to Mumbai!' Vikram shouted as he ran alongside the train. Mallika and Seema waved back until he was out of sight.

Settling into their seats, Mallika asked, 'So you would both like to work for Bhaskar Prabhu after your journalism course is completed?'

'Yeah, very much so,' said Trevor with a big smile.

'Not me, definitely not,' replied Seema. 'I think he is a bit arrogant. I'm not sure I would like to work for him.'

'Arrogant! My God, Seema, do you know how much genuine, worthwhile work this man has done in rural India? He belongs to a rare breed of journalists that one can only aspire to emulate.'

'So what? I don't think I like him much as a person, really. But you seem to adore him so much,' she teased Trevor.

'Don't even dare to make fun of what I think of him.'

Mallika stayed out of the argument between the two friends as she reflected on the two days that had passed by so quickly; and yet, so much seemed to have happened in so little time. For the people in the village, every minute of the day seemed to be about survival. Words like comfort, well-being, and solace were missing from their lives. Something as simple as a Sunday-morning tea enjoyed lazily while reading the newspaper, things that came easily to people like her were taken for granted; such simple joys and pleasurable moments did not even exist for these farmers and their families. When, if ever, did people like Kashibai Sonare, Savitri and Sita Madhe enjoy a meal or a simple relaxing weekend? It was not at all easy to put herself in their shoes and experience life as they experienced it.

After a while, the compartment fell quiet and all of them stretched out on their berths as the train made its way back to Mumbai.

15

EXCHANGING NOTES

Sriram was on the phone when Mallika reached office the day after returning to Mumbai.

'I was just talking to Manoj Rathod. He was very pleased with your visit. How was it? Tell me everything.'

'The visit was good, an eye-opener. It taught me a lot. Most of all, I came to know how much I don't know about our villages and what goes on in the lives of farmers.'

'Well, that is true for almost all of us living in cities, including me. I have thought of a plan. We must go on tour of the villages in Maharashtra, a kind of padayatra.'

'Walking through the villages on foot? Wouldn't that take up too much time? We might cover more area if we use vehicles. Besides, it might be a better idea to tour other parts of India as well, instead of just Maharashtra.'

'That would be too much...wouldn't it?'

'No, I don't think so, not if we plan it well. It's not completely my idea though.'

Sriram looked at Mallika quizzically. 'Where did you get such an idea?'

'From Bhaskar Prabhu.'

'The journalist? Oh! Did you get to meet him before you left for Wardha?'

'No, no, we met in Wardha. We ran into him. Can you believe it? He was taking photographs of a man—a farmer who was digging a well in Kosurla village. Then we accompanied him to visit a family where two women had lost their husbands. He asked them so many questions but took his time about it. I learned so much from that one visit by just listening to him and absorbing his experience and the dignified way in which he interacted with people. Later I asked him for some suggestions for activities that we could undertake and he pointed out that we should visit the poorest districts in other states.'

'That would require very careful planning. We would also need more volunteers.'

'I will get on with that right away and draft a plan. We can go over it in a week.'

'So soon?'

'I am kind of raring to go. I had enough time on the train to think about it.'

'Is this the same Mallika who wanted me to go with her to Wardha?'

Mallika looked up thinking Sriram was teasing her, but he was very serious and continued in the same tone.

'What do you think about politics, Mallika? What if you were asked to join politics?'

'I don't know. I've never thought about it. But this visit to Wardha was such a revelation. I feel more receptive to new ideas now. Why do you ask?'

'Oh, just a thought, a simple question.'

'What are you thinking, Sriram? It can't be just a simple question.'

'Well, during my visit to Yavatmal, on the last night of my stay, I started thinking about how much change and development is required there. It also occurred to me that it would be simplest for the government to do it rather than outsiders like us. I tried to call you then, to talk about this but couldn't reach you.'

He paused and seemed to have concluded but Mallika continued.

'So you think becoming a part of the government is required? Is that why...I mean, are you saying you want to join politics?'

'No, no. In fact, I feel it might all be futile. I have to think about to what extent we would be involved in these activities.'

'Oh! But then, Sriram, what about the plan for the padayatra? Surely, you don't want to cancel it?'

'No, no. Let's work on it as an exploratory approach but only in one state. In Maharashtra. We can come up with an action plan later, after we return. We can review everything then.'

The mixed signals from Sriram were disconcerting for Mallika. But she decided to leave them aside for the time being and focus on planning as he suggested.

'So where should we start, Sriram?'

'First we go from Mumbai to the farthest point in north Maharashtra. From there, I think we could go in a kind of spiral pattern.'

'Spiral pattern? How do you mean?'

'Say we go from Mumbai to Jalgaon or Dhule, from there we walk eastwards through the districts in Vidarbha.'

Mallika brought out a copy of the district map of Maharashtra from her desk drawer and read out from it.

'So Sriram, from Dhule we go to Jalgaon, Buldhana, Akola, Amravati and so on...'

'Exactly. After we go right up to Gondia, we go southwards for a while and turn west again.'

'I think it would actually be southwest, Sriram. This is a kind of triangular spiral.'

'Good, I'm glad we have that agreed on. Will you work on the details? We need to plan our stops and the dates. I will also give you a list of doctors I know from some of these districts.'

'What about places where we don't know anyone?'

'Try to think and figure out Mallika, won't you?' And with his charming but distant smile, Sriram handed over the bulk of the planning to Mallika.

16

THE PARTING

Mallika completed the overall plan and stretched her arms—cat-like—in pleasurable relief. But a sudden thought raised its head from the back of her mind and made her sit up. It was a reminder of the unsatisfying conversation she had had with her parents about her desire to marry Iyer. The uncertainty disconcerted her. She wished she could put her foot down and go ahead with her wish despite their objections. But what had stopped her? On one side was her love for Iyer, her desire to be with him and on the other, her parents' disapproval. Having always obeyed her parents till now, the sudden need to rebel made it all the more difficult to endure the uncertainty. While she was busy working in Wardha, it remained at the back of her mind. But then, she later realized she was not sure how things would be with Iyer now. Her parents' disapproval had brought some change in her. She was wary of that change and the need to come to terms with it. Unconsciously, she had begun to have doubts. The phone rang and she knew instinctively that it would be Iyer.

'When did you return to Mumbai?' he asked in an almost accusatory tone.

'Oh…just yesterday. I did tell you it was a two-day trip. How is your work going?' Mallika replied patiently.

'Why didn't you call me? You have never asked me about my work…strange that you are asking now. And don't change the topic.'

'I would have called you eventually…I mean later today.'

'Eventually? What do you mean by that?'

'Nothing, nothing. I meant I was going to call you today. What are we really arguing about, Iyer?'

'You don't have time to meet as often as we used to. Why are you so preoccupied?'

'But I'm busier now than I was before. I've also been travelling.'

'Let's meet after you finish work.'

'Okay, at six then.'

They walked to the restaurant near her office. They found an empty table and ordered a cup of tea each. Once the waiter left, without a preamble or warning, Iyer took both her hands in his.

'Let's get married.'

'I can't! You know what happened when I brought it up with my parents. I thought we had decided to wait.'

'Well, haven't we waited long enough? Don't you want to get married?'

Mallika was silent.

'Gosh! Have you nothing to say?'

'Iyer, the way my parents reacted has hurt me. Something changed after that. And I can't imagine going against them. I never have before. This has been too stressful for me.'

They quietly finished their teas and called for the bill. Iyer put money on the table quickly and walked out. Mallika was jolted out of her apathy. She ran out of the restaurant and called out to him.

'Iyer, wait, just wait! Look, I care for you. But for some time now, I don't feel... I mean, I don't think getting married and settling down is going to be my priority for now...'

Iyer listened and guilt tugged at her as the colour drained from his fair cheeks.

'Mallika, let's go to my place then for sometime. Let's talk this over. I'll drop you to yours later.'

In order to assuage her guilt, Mallika walked in silence, holding his hand for most of the way till Churchgate station. The silence gave her the strength to speak the truth as they reached a waiting train.

'I don't think we should... I can't come to your place.'

Iyer looked away and then stared ahead grimly.

'As you wish,' he said resignedly and walked straight ahead. Mallika stepped into the ladies compartment and saw Iyer getting into the next one. Beneath his anger, Mallika knew, was a sadness that had grown slowly over the past month as she gradually stopped needing him or even wanting to be with him. She couldn't explain even to herself the aloofness that had come into her. The earlier excitement she had felt at the sound of his voice on the phone, the look in his eyes upon seeing her, her own elation at his inexplicable admiration of her...until only very recently it seemed these things were central to her existence. Should she accept this new change or be saddened by the loss of her passionate feelings? She knew she still cared for Iyer but the romantic magic had somehow disappeared. Mallika squeezed into a seat and on looking up, found Sudha smiling at her.

'You don't jump into running buses now, no?' Both of them laughed.

'I am very careful since that day,' Mallika reassured her and thought how long ago that seemed.

After an awkward silence they smiled at each other again, not really having anything else to talk about. Sudha then remembered something and gestured to her to come closer.

'Remember I told you that I had made a vow that if my housing loan got sanctioned, I would go on vaari, from Alandi to Pandharpur, and make this offering to Vithoba on Ashadhi Ekadashi? And just within two months, the loan got sanctioned! I have now booked a flat. It is small, just a one-room kitchen, but it will be my own.'

Her face glowed with the pride and pleasure as she showed her the offering. Mallika admired the thin gold chain with its leaf-like pendant.

She was not exactly sure what a vaari was except that it was some sort of a pilgrimage.

'So when are you going to Pandharpur?'

'Oh, it is just next week. I thought I would have to wait for a long time for the loan, but it got approved quickly. And the Ashadhi vaari will start next week. So I can go immediately.'

'That must be really nice for you, Sudha. It was good to see you again. I have to get off now at the next station.'

'You are getting down at Dadar?'

'Yes. Okay bye, Sudha.'

'I am also getting down at Dadar today. I have to buy some things.'

The train entered Dadar station and all energies were focussed on the exodus that followed. Mallika and Sudha jumped off the train as it slowed down and were out of the station as the crowds spilled on the platform. They had barely exited the station when a loud noise forced them both to stop and turn around. It sounded like an explosion.

As the train pulled out of the station, bomb explosions had ripped through the ladies compartment and the two compartments adjoining it. Loud screaming and shouting could be heard as people ran out of the station, their faces struck with fear and horror.

'Iyer,' whispered Mallika and shouted out his name as Sudha held her.

Mallika ran back into the station as several others fled out of it. Sudha wouldn't let go of her hand until she told her that she had to go back and find her friend who was in the next compartment. After exchanging phone numbers, Sudha finally relented.

Mallika stood transfixed amidst the noise and mayhem. Most of the train had moved out of the station and stopped. The last compartment was the ladies, from which she had stepped out minutes before. It now stood at the sloping end of the platform. That and two adjoining compartments had their innards torn open. The metal sheets of the coaches were gnarled and twisted, folded like foils of metallic paper. She looked around in a daze but could not see Iyer anywhere. There were bodies and limbs everywhere. And blood. She was rooted to the spot. Ambulance sirens sounded and a rush of activity surrounded her. She was pushed around. She fell. Rising up, she began helping the women who looked like they were injured but able to walk slowly. Men began picking up the injured in pairs or alone and carried them to the waiting ambulances. Some were crying even as they worked to help the injured. Her eyes fell on a mop of dark curls and she rushed to the spot. Two men helped her carry

Iyer outside. Two doctors went from person to person, while attendants were bustling to transfer the injured to an ambulance. The dead remained on the ground. Another ambulance arrived and the one that was filled up, left for the nearest hospital at Parel. The doctor examined Iyer and shook his head. And then Mallika noticed the blood on her clothes and hands. She did not know what was to be done.

There were five other blasts that day on the western railway line within a span of fifteen minutes. This was the first one. The train operations were restored in about six hours. It was close to midnight when Mallika was able to call Sriram. He found her sitting on the footpath next to a body wrapped in a white sheet soiled with dirt and red blotches.

17

A QUESTION OF COMPULSION

Mallika's first instinct was to go back to her parents in Nashik the next morning, but she dismissed the thought and decided to get ready to go to work. Dark circles stared back at her from the bathroom mirror. The phone rang and it was Sudha asking more questions than Mallika had answers for. Mallika told her about Iyer as briefly as she could. After Sriram had come to Dadar station, Iyer's body was taken to his apartment in a taxi. It was wrapped in a dirty cotton bedsheet; Mallika couldn't remember who had given it in the mayhem. Sriram found the key to Iyer's apartment in his back pocket. His wallet, mobile phone and handkerchief were all intact. They called Iyer's family friend in Pondicherry who advised them to cremate David and send the death certificate to him by post. There were no living relatives that he knew of. They took Iyer's body to the Dadar crematorium. It was past three in the morning when Mallika reached her room.

When Sudha called her again the next day to check on her, she suggested in a matter-of-fact manner, 'Come with me next week.'

'What?'

'Come with me to the vaari to Pandharpur. I am going there na, next week,' Sudha continued, quietly but persistently. Mallika asked her for some time to think about it and went to work.

'Sriram, do you know what a vaari is?' Mallika asked when she reached the office.

'Yes, I know. Why do you ask?'

'It starts next week and I'm thinking of going.'

'If you want a short break, maybe you should go visit your parents for a couple of days.'

'No, I don't want to do that. Tell me about vaari. Please.'

'Okay. Pandurang or Vitthal or Vithoba, as you know, is the most revered of deities in Maharashtra, second or equal only to Ganpati. He is actually a folk version of Krishna. You must have heard about the Vitthal Mandir in Pandharpur. Here Pandurang stands alone with his hands on his waist. Nearby is the temple of Rukmini, also called Rakhumai.

'A visit to the Vitthal and Rakhumai temples in Pandharpur is said to bring one closer to self-realization. Other places of pilgrimage promise a place in heaven or to wash away sins, but with vaari, one can eventually attain moksha, so they say. The practice of vaari started from the time of Dnyaneshwar's father or maybe even before that. Over the years, the followers of these saints continued the practice of walking to Pandharpur, singing devotional abhangs in praise of Pandurang all along the way. Today, this journey, or vaari, begins from many places, but the two major ones are: Alandi, the final resting place of Sant Dnyaneshwar, and Dehu, the hometown of Sant Tukaram. It begins about eighteen days before Ashadhi Ekadashi, the eleventh day in the month of Ashadh. That, Mallika, is the basic essence of vaari, though there is much more to it.'

She found it hard to believe that Sudha actually meant she would go on foot, on an eighteen-day journey to Pandharpur. But the next thing Sriram said was even more unbelievable.

'I've gone on vaari twice from Alandi.'

Mallika stared back at him open-mouthed. Someone like Sriram, who was so engrossed in his work at Care People, sparing any of his time for something like a pilgrimage was beyond her imagination. Staying completely away from his work and for so many days!

'Are you serious? And what about your patients?'

'My patients had to deal with my absence.'

'So, tell me more. When did you go?'

'The first time, I went reluctantly, only because I had promised a friend I would be part of the doctors' volunteer group that had organized medical camps for varkaris along the route to Pandharpur. Then, I went again two years later in place of another volunteer who had to cancel the trip at the last minute. But since then, I haven't gone because of other commitments. It's been eleven years now since the first time I went. It is a good way to feel rejuvenated and energized.'

'But you have never mentioned it before.'

'You never asked me before. As you say, it is not a small thing. But it is also not to be treated like a great achievement. Vaari is essentially meant to be a pleasurable routine for regular participants. Like the change of seasons. One does it out of a sense of compulsion. It's nothing to boast about. So, are you thinking of going on this journey?

I have a friend in Alandi who takes a group every year and you could go with them next year if you like.'

To Mallika it seemed like destiny, as if she was meant to go on vaari.

'Well, this is rather unexpected. But I will at least go to Alandi. I really think I should go, though I don't know how it will be.'

'But why this sudden urge?'

Mallika told Sriram about her first meeting with Sudha and her being there again yesterday. She also told him about Sudha's vow.

After a long pause, Sriram asked, 'But why do you want to go?'

'I feel it will ease the pain of losing my friend... of what happened yesterday. Can you understand that?'

'Maybe. But let's keep that aside for now. There is too much to do right now, the planning for our journey, the draft plan we discussed just yesterday... You said you were raring to go on the tour. We have to finalize the volunteers. Or have you forgotten?'

'No, I haven't forgotten. But I want to go for this vaari first.'

'You could go next year.'

'No, I must go this time, next week.'

'I can order you not to go. You will be taking leave from work. I can't allow that at this juncture.'

Mallika looked at him a little dazed. He was being firm and yet he was not harsh. This new side of Sriram surprised her. Or did it? Hadn't she seen a glimpse of it when she first met him, at her first interview when she had walked out, unable to answer or even address his questions? But then, his phone call the next day had changed everything. He was like a kind and understanding teacher during her first few days at the job. A part of her wanted to do as he told her. But she could not forget Iyer's face, his disappointment and anger and how she felt that this journey would help her come to terms with the feeling of guilt about him. That feeling made her stubbornly push ahead.

'But I have made up my mind to go.'

'Don't you realize that the padayatra is more important? You are being adamant. Doesn't it seem like a silly whim to go on this vaari when we have a more important task on hand?'

'It is *not* a silly whim. I have to go, I must go.'

Sriram glared at her and she stared back at him. A long silence followed. Mallika finally looked away, looked down at her hands, and Sriram sighed.

'Go then.'

That was the last they spoke of the subject that day. The next day, Sriram gave Mallika his friend's address in Alandi and some directions on how to reach his house from the railway station.

Meanwhile, he was to take a train that afternoon to Amravati in preparation for the padayatra and had brought his usual olive-green backpack that he took everywhere. Mallika stood in silence, feeling guilty about not listening to him.

'Okay then. I'm leaving now. You stay with the Professor's group all through the vaari. Don't wander or get lost among the crowds.'

'Yes,' said Mallika as he shook her hand and then, in a quick movement, hugged her.

'Take care,' he whispered, as he turned and walked away before Mallika could thank him. Her mind was preoccupied with a new anticipation as she prepared to go on this journey with thousands of others.

18

THE TEMPLE SPIRE

It was after ten in the morning when Sudha and Mallika reached Professor Bharadwaj's house in Alandi. The retired physics teacher was Sriram's friend. Curlicued ferns and tongue-like anthuriums of deep carmine spilled out of red clay pots bordering the cottage's narrow veranda, where two grey-haired men sat in cane chairs. Sudha and Mallika removed their footwear and kept them near a shoe-rack overflowing with chappals and shoes. Inside, cotton satranjis patterned in bright blue, purple and green bands were spread out on the floor. Men sat in semi-circles around an array of snacks. Plates and spoons were scattered around the heaps of bananas, bowls of laddoos and potato chivda. Mallika wondered if all these people had come to join the vaari like them. The Professor welcomed her with a namaste and, turning towards the passageway, called out: 'Aga, are you listening?'

In a moment his wife appeared, wiping her wet hands on the pallu of her sari. She wore traditional seven-pearl earrings, a red bindi and her hair was in a neat, long, grey plait. Her features seemed almost identical to that of her husband. She smiled at Sudha and looked at Mallika from head to toe, filled with maternal love, as the Professor introduced them. She took Mallika's hand and led her and Sudha inside to a square kitchen, where three women were peeling boiled potatoes, washing bunches of green, leafy methi, and winnowing puffed rice.

Further down the passage in another room, older women were resting on iron beds, their varied positions reflecting in the mirror of the Godrej steel cupboard facing the door. The two other rooms had no furniture; the floor was covered with maroon satranjis, old and worn, compared to the bright, new and thick cotton ones in the hall laid out for the men. As in the hall, here too, steel thalis containing bananas and dry snacks were placed in the centre. A young boy brought in tea for everyone. Sudha and Mallika sat down cross-legged next to a group of young and middle-aged women, all of whom greeted them with smiles. A young woman introduced the others to them, explaining each one's relationship with the Professor and his wife. They were relatives or friends of the host couple, or the friend of a relative or the relative of a friend. All were there to join the vaari, though very few planned to go all the way to Pandharpur. Many were from Pune and were to accompany the palkhi from Alandi up to their city. They were all curious about the two newcomers.

'How far are you going?'

'We are going up to Pandharpur,' Sudha spoke for the two of them and told them about her vow and home loan. Then they turned to Mallika.

She hesitated to tell them about Iyer, but their silence and expectant eyes nudged her into confessing. Tears started flowing from her eyes as she told them about the loss of her dear friend. They of course knew about the multiple explosions on the trains in Mumbai. The young woman next to Mallika put her arm around her shoulder. Another lady consoled her. Unable to deal with all the emotions, Mallika excused herself.

Everyone in the house was talking about the journey which was to begin tomorrow. By evening, nearly a hundred thousand devotees of Vitthal arrived in Alandi. Dindis— batches of varkaris from parts of Maharashtra and the neighbouring states of Karnataka, Andhra Pradesh and Madhya Pradesh—had congregated in the town. An old royal family from Ankali in Karnataka had lent horses for the palkhi. Devotional songs were ringing out with calls to Vitthal, Pandurang, Dnyaneshwar Mauli and Tukaram.

On the next day, the eighth day of the lunar month of Jyeshtha, the palkhi, a palanquin carrying Sant Dnyaneshwar's paduka, would be placed in a chariot and leave Alandi for Pandharpur. An elderly woman at the Professor's house said that the vaari is no different from children returning to their anxious mothers in the evening after being out at play all day. The preliminaries for the journey would begin that night at the temple. Sudha and Mallika went to the temple with the other women to attend the kirtans and aarti at the Dnyaneshwar Mandir and returned late. The final preparations for the journey were to begin the next day in the temple, long before dawn.

It was quarter to four when Mallika woke up to the sound of temple bells. It reminded her of the day of Diwali when her mother would wake them all up to have their baths before sunrise. As she sat up, three women were already draping their saris and two others were combing their hair.

Sudha and Mallika too got ready for the day. Deep in her heart, Mallika was glad she had agreed to come here with Sudha. She knew the thought of Iyer and his brutal death would raise its head in her mind every now and then. But the activities planned for the days ahead would, she hoped, insulate her from the grief. It was not only the grief of losing Iyer but the way they parted that troubled her more. Enough, do not dwell on these thoughts, she told herself, as they walked to the temple in groups of three and four.

After a half hour of the bells ringing out in the early morning, the Kakad Aarti began. The men and women gathered in the large temple hall sang in unison, offering paeans to many deities and saints. One song followed another as if they had known these songs from birth. Sudha was engrossed, eyes shut and singing along. Mallika felt like the odd one out until her neighbour opened a palm-sized booklet and pointed out the lyrics to her.

When the final song was sung, the bells touched a crescendo of pure reverberation. There was a constant flow of people in and out of the temple. Mallika waited outside while Sudha and the others returned to the Professor's house. A man wearing a badge asked Mallika if she wanted anything. He was one of the four hundred volunteers who kept the temple clean during this time every year and helped the lakhs of visitors on the vaari. He told her that the crowd of people would ebb for a while at 2:30 in the afternoon when the sanctum sanctorum closed for the priests to wash Mauli's idol and drape it with new clothes. Fascinated by all the activity, she stayed back and watched for a little longer.

At three in the afternoon, two white horses, arrayed in ceremonial red cloth with golden tassels, entered the

temple premises. One horse was for Mauli and the other
for an escort rider. Twenty-seven dindis marched ahead of
the palkhi and twenty dindis followed, entering the temple
complex one after another. Each dindi was a group made
up of twenty to forty varkaris. While all the men wore
white—a dhoti or a loose cotton pyjama, a tunic and a
topi—the women wore saris in bright reds, greens, blues,
yellows, or purples. In each dindi group, one man carried a
stringed veena, while another hoisted the pataka, a saffron
coloured flag shaped like a horizontal 'M'. One woman
carried a pot of the tulsi plant and another a pot of water
for people who felt thirsty during the journey. For each of
these men and women, it was an honour to carry out their
function and duty.

Meanwhile, the banks of the Indrayani thronged with
varkaris. The river rejoiced at the arrival of her annual
visitors, embracing them with her many arms. Mallika
watched the men and women play like children. Forming
circles, they clapped hands together in a game of zhimma.
Then in pairs, they held each other's hands tightly and spun
around for phugdi, gathering speed and matching the taal
was mrudunga rhythms and chants of 'Gyanba-Tukaram,
Gyanba-Tukaram'. She walked aimlessly and once again
reached the temple, the centre of all activity.

The temple was decorated with strings of flowers. The
main doorways of the main hall, the Veena Mandap, were
festooned with radiant marigold. At four-thirty, the chief
trustee of the Alandi Sansthan brought Mauli's paduka
out to the Veena Mandap and placed them reverently in
the palkhi. Besides the temple trustees, many other public
officials were present: officers of the district rural police,

the state minister of tourism, and the master of ceremonies. The honour of lifting the palkhi first belongs to the people of Alandi. Four men selected for the occasion received a ceremonial coconut and bowed their heads to Mauli's samadhi, where Sant Dnyaneshwar had gone into a terminal state of meditation. Amidst chants of 'Pundalika varada hari Vitthal', they lifted the palkhi. They circumambulated the temple in a clockwise direction before taking the palkhi outside, marking the first step of the journey to Pandharpur.

As the palkhi departed, all eyes went up to the temple spire. According to an ancient legend, it is believed that the spire quivers in anticipation of the divine meeting of Dnyaneshwar Mauli with Vitthal.

The people of Alandi set off firecrackers to celebrate the commencement of the journey. The procession traversed slowly as people jostled for a chance to behold Mauli's paduka with their own eyes. At about eight in the evening, the palkhi reached the home of Mauli's grandparents near the temple, where it remained for the night. The evening ended with an aarti.

When Mallika went back to the Professor's house, she found everyone assembled in the front room, waiting for her. 'So late you are. Don't wander about like this,' Sudha whispered to her as the Professor welcomed them rather formally.

'Welcome to my home everyone. Early in the morning tomorrow, we will leave for Pandharpur. We are not part of any "official" dindi, but we too will follow in the same disciplined manner: walk all the way, live in modest lodgings and eat simple, rationed food.'

Professor Bharadwaj then introduced Sudha and Mallika

to the rest of the group. There were two Physics teachers, a young couple, Madhu and Vivek Chavan, who lived in London but came to Alandi for the vaari each year; a German Professor of Indology and expert on the Bhakti movement, Dr Alban Dietrich; an American research student Amy Joseph, studying for a term at the University of Pune; and a software engineer from Bangalore, taking the journey for the second consecutive year. Swati Shiledar, a young reporter with the *Pune Kesari*, a Marathi newspaper, was also there to cover the vaari for her paper for the first time. Every evening she was to dispatch her report with a summary of the day's events.

The group was to reach Pune tomorrow—the only major city on the itinerary of villages and towns. Swati told Mallika that the local newspapers in Pune had already published information on the facilities available for varkaris, the various sponsors for their stay and meals, the route for the palkhi procession in the city, the no-traffic zones and the alternate routes, in order to avoid any hindrance in the pilgrims' journey.

19

THE SILENCE

The group left Alandi at six in the morning and, after walking for two hours, reached an enormous arch adorned with flowers to welcome the palkhi and the varkaris. Huge crowds of people lined the road and a group of officials led by the Rural Development Minister of Maharashtra came forward with garlands. The mayor and municipal commissioner of Pimpri-Chinchwad were also present to receive the palkhi. Men, women and children waited in anticipation of catching a glimpse of the silver paduka; only a lucky few could manage to get close to the palkhi.

The palkhi of Sant Tukaram from Dehu was also on its way to Pune, ahead of the procession. Born two centuries after Dnyaneshwar, Sant Tukaram and the beloved Mauli never met during their lifetimes, but their palkhis crossed paths every year in Pune. They left Pune together to part again, taking different routes, both leading to Pandharpur.

Mallika asked the Professor if there was a deeper meaning to this; two of the greatest devotees of Vitthal going their separate ways to reach the same destination. He gave a wry smile and said, 'No such thing, Mallika. The palkhis used to travel together until some years ago. But disagreements of some sort flared up between the organizers. So, for practical purposes, the two formed separate routes.'

The palkhis reached Wakdewadi in Pune at about five in the evening, where the Mayor and Municipal Commissioner of Pune along with other government officials welcomed them—there were going to be government officials as they entered each town and village. People from office buildings along the road were also watching the procession. Devoid of vehicles, roads covered with colourful rangolis awaited the procession. When the palkhis slowed down for the people, varkaris indulged in games of phugdi and sang bharudas. The air reverberated with the chant of 'Gyanba-Tukaram' and the rhythmic ring of the cymbals. Sudha, Swati, Mallika and the rest got drawn into the boundless energy, eventually pairing off and spinning like the varkaris. The doctor couple also joined in while the four professors watched.

The palkhi then proceeded to the Agriculture College chowk. A large number of the varkaris were farmers, who had joined the vaari after their first sowing around monsoon. Organizations and committees welcomed the varkaris throughout its route. The ruling political party, the INP, distributed laddoos and oranges, while its main opponent, the BNP, distributed packets of puri-bhaji and bananas. Volunteers of the Anti-Corruption People's Movement presented the varkaris with stainless steel plates, bowls and spoons. Numerous other groups distributed tea, toothbrushes, rubber slippers, first-aid kits and camping equipment.

'Local branches of nearly all political parties, their youth and women's wings welcome the varkaris to Pune and distribute items of daily needs in a well-orchestrated manner, their political rivalries forgotten for the moment,' Swati noted in her report for the day.

The palkhis reached the Dnyaneshwar Paduka Mandir and Tukaram Paduka Mandir on Fergusson College Road at eight-thirty that evening. Crowds gathered for aartis at both temples, while the palkhis made slow progress to take up temporary residence in the heart of the city. For the whole of the next day, the Dnyaneshwar palkhi would be at the Palkhi Vithoba Mandir in Bhawani Peth while the Tukaram Palkhi would be housed at the Nivdungya Vithoba Mandir in Nana Peth.

Professor Bharadwaj took his group to Narayan Peth, where he had arranged for them to stay the night. Early next morning, Swati and Mallika walked to the Vithoba Mandir at Nana Peth where the mahapuja had already begun. After photographing the temple and varkaris, they explored the city looking for news-worthy stories and interesting titbits. Again, they found a lot of organizations arranging meals and free services like health check-up camps, barber services, footwear repairs, umbrella repairs, tailoring, letter-writing, distribution of prayer books (*Haripaath*), hot water and even soap for the varkaris to bathe.

At six the next morning, the palkhis left Pune after an aarti. Three hours later, at Hadapsar, they embarked on their separate routes: the Dnyaneshwar palkhi southwards to Saswad; and the Tukaram palkhi eastwards to Loni Kalbhor. Sudha told Mallika that the two palkhis would meet again fifteen days later and cover the final short distance to Pandharpur together.

Going through the procession and talking to numerous

people with Swati, Mallika was amazed to find thousands of pilgrims not only from different parts of Maharashtra but also from other states like Andhra Pradesh, Karnataka, Gujarat, Madhya Pradesh, Tamil Nadu, Kerala and even Rajasthan. Perhaps even more amazing was the order and discipline everyone seemed to instinctively abide by. A fixed routine was followed every day: at dawn, the silver padukas were worshipped in their tent. A conch shell sounded the wake-up call three times every ten minutes. On the first call, the varkaris gathered their belongings and got ready for the day. The palkhi with the silver paduka was placed in the chariot by the palkhi officials. On the second call, the varkaris stood in the dindi at the appointed places. Each dindi was led by the flag bearer, followed by men in rows of two or three. In the centre of these rows stood the mrudung player, his drum hanging on a sturdy rope around his shoulder. The veena player stood at the end. After the rows of men, the women followed with the potted tulsi perched on their heads, along with the requisite pots of water. All other groups followed the numbered dindis. Mallika and the others stood among them, led by Professor Bharadwaj. On the third call of the conch shell, the procession marched ahead to the chants of 'Jai jai Ram Krishna Hari', 'Jai jai Pandurang Hari', 'Jai Hari Vitthal', and 'Dnyanba Tukaram'.

At noon, they reached the Urlidev temple for a short rest. A medical check-up station had been set up there by a team of forty volunteer doctors. A volunteer from a local newspaper distributed jaggery laddoos. Everyone threw themselves on the grass near the temple grounds, exhausted yet flushed with joy. Mallika was now used to the routine of walking from morning till sunset with only three short stops in between. She felt that fifteen more days of the same may grow monotonous and wondered if she had made a mistake by coming. Maybe I should have listened to Sriram and stayed back to plan the padayatra, she thought as she opened a packet of sweet laddoos. The Professor called for their attention.

'Okay, the picnic is now over. The hardest part of the journey begins today. We have to climb a rough, uphill road, and I strongly advise that everyone should sling their bags onto the back and shoulders and keep their hands free. If you have brought a raincoat or waterproof jacket, slip it on.'

Everyone meekly obeyed and joined the long march of the pilgrims. The farmers from the village had lent twenty bullock carts to ease the way for the palkhi chariot through the Dive Ghat stretch, which wound through hilly terrain. Many others clamoured to donate their bullock carts, too, but they could be accommodated. Arguments broke out, leaving many men disappointed. Elders among the palkhi officials did their best to pacify them and cool tempers. The group walked along and passed the first turn on the uphill road. The chanting of 'Dnyanba, Tukaram' and singing had not stopped at any time during the climb. As they took the second turn of the ghat, the skies burst and the pilgrims hailed 'Vitthal, Vitthal' in great jubilation. They all thanked Professor Bharadwaj for warning them about the sudden rains.

On the third turn of the ghat, there was a problem negotiating the bullock carts on the uphill slopes. With twenty carts linked together in a long stretch, it made for a very rough ride. One bullock broke free and tried to escape.

One of the varkaris was slightly injured in the chaos that followed. To everyone's relief, two dindi managers and a few young men grabbed hold of the bullock and forcefully returned it to the cart.

Ahead of all this commotion, the other varkaris crossed the main ghat section, chanting verses from Haripaath, followed by the abhangas. Hills, green from the rain, stood in splendid welcome as the entire contingent of dindis and other groups of people clambered up. One by one, the extra bullock carts were disengaged, until only the original four remained. On the summit of the ghat, villagers from the surrounding areas gathered to marvel at the spectacle of so many joyful people moving through their hills.

It was four in the afternoon when the procession completed the crossing of the entire ghat section. At Zendewadi, Swati and Mallika stretched out flat on a little patch of verdant grass, a little away from the rest of the group. They were forced to get up when the dindis gathered to walk again, and soon they were all marching to the chanting of 'Gyanba, Tukaram' resonating in the hills.

They reached Saswad in the evening for a two-day stopover, giving Mallika a chance to better acquaint herself with the others in the group. Just as he had done in Pune, here too, Professor Bharadwaj had procured two rooms in a flat. He had made several friends over the years along the vaari route.

'I have not seen you before in our vaari group,' said Dr Dietrich to Mallika, adjusting his thick glasses. He sat next to her on the woven cane mat spread out on the floor.

'Dr Dietrich, this is the first time I have come for vaari,' responded Mallika.

'Hmm. Well, for me it is the hundredth time.'

She stared at him and he laughed aloud, drawing Professor Bharadwaj over to them. 'Mallika, he does this to every first-timer. And every time it has the same effect.'

Dr Dietrich told Mallika, 'I have gone many times from Dehu to Pandharpur. I have a friend in Pune, a poet and author and, ah...what shall I say? He does many other things, film direction, documentaries, etc. I went with this friend to Dehu and then onwards to Pandharpur. Then for some years I made the trip alone. Five years ago, I met Professor Bharadwaj and now I go from Alandi to Pandharpur every year.'

'That must be such an enriching experience. I was not even aware of vaari and varkaris until some months ago. My friend Sudha was to come on this journey, and I decided to join her after I lost a friend in the recent blasts in Mumbai.'

She stopped talking the moment she sensed tears rising. Dr Dietrich looked at her and seemed to understand.

'Yes, but you and I are simple, ordinary people. We are just a small part of a long history of vaari. You know, according to my friend, the world as seen by Tukaram, the poet, is of relevance even today. The faith of people like Tukaram is rooted in the earth as a spiritual entity. It is the same for the varkaris. Do you know how Vitthal the diety originated and came to stand on a brick in the temple at Pandharpur?'

'I remember hearing it from my grandmother, but it is a bit hazy now so please, tell me the story.'

'Well, Pundalik was a young man who got married and was so devoted to his wife that he ended up neglecting his parents. When they wished to go to Kashi for pilgrimage, he dragged them there, tied to a rope. On the way to Kashi, a learned sage explained to Pundalik the importance of caring for one's parents and Pundalik soon changed his attitude. Once again, he took his parents for their pilgrimage to Kashi, this time taking good care of them, and returned to Pandharpur. He remained devoted to his old parents and looked after them diligently from then onwards. Pleased with his devotion, Lord Vishnu decided to visit him at his home. Pundalik was busy serving his parents and pushed a brick towards him, telling Lord Vishnu to wait on it till he finished his work. Lord Vishnu stood on the brick and waited, his hands resting on his waist on either side. When Pundalik met him, Vishnu wished to grant him a boon. Pundalik said, "The way you are standing before me, I only ask that you stand before your devotees this way forever."

'This is how Pandurang, the deity, originated in Pandharpur and stands there till this day. Hands on his waist with elbows pointed out, he waits for devotees to come and meet him. The varkaris have the same intense devotion towards him as Pundalik had towards his parents. But there is a strong parallel here. The varkaris are mostly farmers. They first finish sowing their crops and then take the vaari to Pandharpur. You see, they too, fulfill their earthly duties first before affirming their devotion to their diety. So the bhakti of Pundalik and that of the varkaris has a strong bond with their faith in earthly life. They do not leave one for the sake of the other. There is much that I have come to learn over the years from the vaari. These stories, legends and lifelong beliefs compel us pilgrims to think and dwell on the real meaning behind the obvious and learn lessons for life.'

'One of the first things I noticed was that people mingle and walk together in the procession but keep to their discipline and routine for everything.'

'You're right, Mallika. But have you noticed something else? It is people in power and authority who are at the forefront at an official occasion. The mayors, commissioners, and ministers will lead the reception party in any village or town that we pass through. If the vaari is a procession of ordinary people, farmers, cowherds, why should an ordinary citizen from the village or town not welcome them? This pompous show of authority is the worst in Pandharpur.'

'How so, Dr Dietrich?'

'You know who performs the puja at the temple there?'

'The Mayor of Pandharpur?'

'No. The Chief Minister of Maharashtra! They include a couple of varkaris as well in the puja. But why should a man who has not walked like them or with them be the one to lead this prayer ritual? It is ridiculous and so unfair.'

Mallika nodded in agreement.

Swati interrupted and passed on her laptop to Mallika to read a report while Dr Dietrich walked away. Swati nudged her, 'Read, read.'

Saswad has a limited municipal water supply. But the people of this town had determined months earlier that they would not let this be a problem for the varkaris. For two months water was supplied only thrice a week, thus saving water. The saved water is now supplied by the municipality to the varkaris through thirty-five tankers. Similarly, health and hygiene is also given due attention. The town sponsors lunch for the varkaris, while the 'Varkari Seva Mandal' from London has sponsored an

eye health camp, with free eye check-ups. Free spectacles
are also distributed to those who need them. The varkaris
were welcomed to Saswad by the Mayor and the Deputy
Mayor.

Just as she finished reading, Mallika spotted a woman who
looked very familiar. She followed her and tapped on her
shoulder. The woman turned around but quickly pulled
the sari pallu over her head and started walking even
faster. Mallika was sure she had seen her before and kept
following her. The woman turned around and ran. Mallika
then decided not to pursue her but to seek her out later.

The next morning, they left Saswad and headed for
Jejuri, the famous temple town. They reached the village
border of Yamaai Shivari at eleven and stopped for lunch.
Like many others, they sat in the shade of a tree that
Professor Bharadwaj had spotted and were thankful for the
respite from the strong sun. Their packed lunch comprised
bhakri and a mixed bhaji of brinjal, potatoes and fenugreek
leaves. The first bite of green chillies had Mallika and several
others reaching for their water bottles. Professor Bharadwaj
laughed at their plight and opened up a tupperware box full
of morsel-sized groundnut and jaggery laddoos. Everyone
took one and bit into the sweet to soothe their burning
tongues.

Later Dr Dietrich told Mallika about the beauty of Arun
Kolatkar's poetry and the collection of poems named after the
town. All these interesting nuggets from the learned Indologist
only enriched Mallika's experience. Jejuri, the temple town
of Khandoba, was resounding with the clamorous hailing
of 'Yalkot, Yalkot, Jai Malhar'. A staggering seventeen
kilometres had been covered to get there. Men and women

formed separate pairs to play phugdi, holding hands and spinning in clockwise and anti-clockwise directions. Professor Bharadwaj took Dr Dietrich's hands and, ignoring his protests, began to spin. Swati and Mallika had a quick go at it, stopping only when their heads began to reel. Clouds threatened to tear open and pour down on them but the cool evening breeze drove them away. At 6:30 p.m., after the aarti, they retired for the day, happily exhausted.

The next morning Swati took Mallika on a photography expedition. She asked the varkaris politely for permission before clicking their pictures. An old woman was gathering stones to weigh down a sari spread out on the grass to dry. Swati handed Mallika the camera and helped her. Mallika clicked candid photographs of them working together. As she watched them through the camera lens, a strange feeling overwhelmed her. She remembered that she hadn't thought of Iyer even once during these past few days. She felt guilty, distressed. Her life before this journey seemed like a distant memory. As she walked in silence she realized that this was no longer just Sudha carrying out her vow and her tagging along. It had become her journey. The vaari is mine, she thought, but I cannot fathom the apprehension I feel about the coming days. What will happen when we walk through Valhe, Lonand, Taradgaon, Phaltan, Barad, Natepute, Malshiraz, Velapur, Shegaon, and Wakhri?

On the way to Taradgaon, at Chandobacha Limba, the first Ubhe Ringan, or the 'vertical gathering', was to take place. At three in the afternoon, the procession reached the venue led by Mauli's horse, followed by another horse and rider. Fifty varkaris ran behind the two horses, while others formed two long rows leaving space for the horses to pass through. They chanted and swayed to the rhythm of 'Gyanaba, Tukaram'. The varkaris raised their flags high as Mauli's horse galloped towards the palkhi and the horseback rider following it raised his flag higher. The two horses rode ahead, while the varkaris ran along the path, calling out, 'Mauli, Mauli!' In a while, Mauli's horse stopped and turned back, bowing its head at the palkhi. A man garlanded the horse and fed it a handful of walnuts and cashews. As it trotted back through the rows of dindis behind the palkhi chariot, the varkaris showered the honoured horse with bukka, a black ceremonial powder that is applied on the forehead as a small dot. Marking the end of the Ubhe Ringan, everybody jumped high, chanting in unison, 'Viththal, Vitthal, Vitthal, Vitthal!' Soon they proceeded to Taradgaon where the community aarti announced the end of the day.

At Lonand, Swati interviewed two police officials and they discussed the security arrangements for the procession during the vaari period: a special team managing the traffic to minimize congestion problems and police constables keeping watch for petty thieves and pickpockets. Swati noted down the officials' names but they asked her not to use it in the article.

'All this is in service of the varkaris. We cannot leave our jobs to join in this journey. But the varkaris do this every year, so at least helping them is our way of taking part in the pilgrimage.'

On the twelfth day of the vaari, Sudha and Mallika sat together watching a group of the varkaris singing. Sudha held Mallika's hand in hers and patted it, 'I am so happy you came with me.'

'Yes, I am too.'

'Look at them. They are so completely immersed in their devotion of Vitthal. They have left all their worldly worries behind them. Their hearts must be so light.'

'In anticipation of reaching Pandharpur?'

'Yes. But also just being on this journey. The journey is more important than the glimpse of their deity in Pandharpur, you know?'

There was an eerie silence and spirits were dampened when two men breathed their last during the lunch break on the way to Phaltan. An eighty-year-old man died of heart failure, and the other, sixty-five-year-old, died while taking a nap after lunch. Everyone agreed that the two men were indeed fortunate to have died during vaari, for that meant they were already with their beloved Vitthal.

In Solapur district, the lady sarpanch of Dharmapuri and other officials welcomed the palkhi procession with the same gusto as in the places that they had crossed earlier.

The next day, the procession reached the Dhava-Bavi mound in the afternoon as the varkaris sang the abhanga 'Sinchana karita moola, Vruksha olaave sakala'. Which meant that when the roots are watered well, the entire tree is nourished.

Following the melodious song, the managers called out the dindi numbers one by one and the varkaris ran down the hilly slope chanting, 'Mauli, Mauli!'

Professor Bharadwaj turned to Mallika, who was watching everything intently, 'Mallika, folklore tell us that when Sant Tukaram reached this hilly slope hundreds of years ago, he saw the temple dome in Pandharpur, even from this distance. His devotion attained such a peak at that moment that he ran down the slope to speed up his progress. The varkaris now follow this tradition, called dhava, which as you know simply means...'

'Run!'

When it was their turn, they charged down the slope.

After that energetic dash down the hill, they rested on the grass in the open countryside where folk artists sang a bharuda with soul-stirring lyrics tinged with humour and irony. One singer recited scenes from the joys and sorrows of everyday life. Men, women, and children listened in rapt attention. Some women formed small circles and danced gracefully while others sang couplets called ovi, a union of prose and verse. No break was complete without a round of phugdi. So the women paired up and played until they felt forced to break apart and hold their heads to stop the dizzying and spinning feeling. The other women laughed, one of them rather loudly. She was the same woman Mallika had chased after earlier. Mallika went and sat next to her and held her wrist as she tried to get up.

'I remember you. You are Sita Madhe from Kosurla village near Wardha, ho na?' Mallika asked her in Marathi.

She was silent for a while and then whispered 'hao' in her Varahdi dialect.

She now sat more comfortably, stretching her legs out a little and resting her elbows on her raised knees. When her sari pallu dropped from her head, she ignored it.

'Have you run away?' Mallika ask her cautiously.

'Tu kon lagli majhi, asla ichraya?' Who are you to me, to ask me such questions?

'Chhoti bahin, Savitri saarkhi.' A younger sister, Mallika told her, like Savitri. At the mention of her sister-in-law, she looked at Mallika. Her eyes flashed angrily, reminding Mallika of the way Savitri had raged when they had met her.

'Who are you to ask me anything? What makes you think I can run away from the miserable life back in my village? The perpetual work to heat the hearth, the toiling in mud...the constant need for money and the gaping lecherous avarice of that haraamkhor...saalaa...' Mallika silently listened to her abusing the moneylender.

'This vaari is just an excuse for me to get away for a few days. I will have to go back there. I was like Savitri, too, when I was younger. Full of energy and anger, ready to fight any adversity, to work hard and rise against the world. But now I'm older and have seen much more hardship and sorrow than she has.' She paused.

'How can I leave her alone to fend for the children, hers and mine? I will go back. I have not told her anything but she will understand that I have not gone forever.'

Mallika merely watched her in silence, wondering how to apologize for having offended her.

In a calmer tone, Sita added, 'A group of people from my village have come for the vaari. I have come with them. Savitri will figure it out I'm sure, as she knows me and understands our common angst.'

Mallika felt humbled and regretted questioning her. Patronizing, yes, that was the tone of my questioning, she thought, just because she is poor and possibly semi-literate. Not knowing how to make amends, she simply held Sita's wrist again, which prompted Sita to ask, 'Kaaon pori? kaay zhala tula?' Why girl, what's happened to you?

Before she could think of anything to say, Sita asked, 'Ani tu hitha kaay karun rahili?' And what are you doing here?

'I've come to see what the vaari is all about.'

'Ekti?'

'No, I am with a small group. Just like you!'

She laughed. Standing up quickly, Sita walked away, leaving Mallika amazed at her strength.

They were now only a few nights away from Pandharpur, the last lap of the journey. Mallika walked with the others in silence. Oblivious to everything around her, she was not in control of her movements. She felt a sudden release from the world. People floated away. There was emptiness. There was silence. She was free. She watched everything go by and in a moment she saw a light so intense and brilliant that she felt blinded. She wanted to close her eyes. Silence spread all around her like the light. Why has everything changed? How has all this happened? What is now unfolding? The questions floated and dissolved in the light until there was no thought.

After a while, it all began to change. Mallika slowly began to see the men and women, all looking the same and yet a little different somehow. She smiled. This is all a game, she thought. A game started at the beginning of the universe. The world created with little parts of some divinity or perhaps just energy, with creatures living as they were meant to be; short, simple, straight lives from birth to death. Killing, eating, procreating and finally dying. Not satisfied with this quick, simple game, men and women were created and left to fend for themselves, scattered all around the world. They were thrown into the world to realize their true purpose. Is that the ultimate aim of the game? For all creatures to realize their origin and return to it? It would have been easy enough with only the body and the soul. So the stakes are pushed higher. Minds are added and filled with passion. Then come egos and vanities, with anger and frustration close behind. Greed and desire follow as lust, jealousy and hatred rush in.

In ignorance, men and women walk into the world with these little invisible stones and boulders tied to their hands and legs. Walk into the jungles and try to find your way back to where you came from originally, is the only rule they must remember. But the moment they are put on earth, they forget just that. They only tend to the stones and boulders. They get completely engrossed in polishing and sharpening the worthless stones to use against each other, and in the process push themselves further away from the point to which they should return. It all seems clear now.

Suddenly, Mallika could feel drops of water fall on her cheeks and forehead. A few more drops made her open her eyes and instinctively hold up a hand against the sun, and find curious faces gazing at her. In an instant she sat up. A woman held her hand and said, 'Too much exertion for you.'

People had gathered around her. She stood up quickly saying, 'I am feeling alright now.' Everyone scattered back to the procession and the rhythmic chanting of Dhyanba, Tukaram continued. She could think only of the light that had engulfed her earlier and felt a sense of calm descend upon her like never before.

Her reverie was broken when a woman sitting close by started singing an abhanga of Sant Soyrabai:

Aavagha ranga ek jala, Rangi rangala sriranga
metu pana gele vaya, pahata pandharichya raya.

All the colours of the world have merged into one,
    Sriranga rejoices in the colours
The feeling of you and I is lost on seeing the Lord of
    Pandharpur.

She then realized that no one from her group was around. Walking through the procession, while trying to find her bearings, she scanned the crowd until she spotted Swati photographing a group of schoolchildren.

'Where were you, Mallika? Here, take a picture of me with the kids. Were you lost?'

'Well, I'm found now,' she replied.

When they rejoined the group Mallika told Professor Bharadwaj that she had to return to Mumbai immediately.

'But, so suddenly? Is anything wrong, did something happen?

'No, Professor. But I must get back right away. Something urgent has come up.'

'Alright. Come with me then.'

She said a hurried goodbye to the others.

Dr Dietrich came forward to shake hands with her. 'I hope I see you again, maybe next year?'

'Maybe,' she mumbled.

Swati looked at her a little bewildered. Mallika hugged her and said, 'We'll meet again. Keep in touch.'

Sudha asked no questions. She seemed to say, 'I know you have found peace and now you must go and do your work.'

The Professor arranged for a ride for Mallika to Solapur railway station in a Tata Sumo jeep with a few other people. Mallika was to take a train from Solapur to Mumbai, or a bus, if that was easier. She slid into the empty seat just behind the driver. The man sitting next to her had his head flopped back and was snoring away. Dropping her backpack between them, she inched closer to the window and rested her head as the jeep gathered speed.

A thud and a sudden jerk woke her up. There was commotion outside. A man forced open the driver's door and dragged him out. More men appeared and started beating the driver. The vehicle had hit an autorickshaw. The others in the jeep sat motionless, looking out of the window. The man next to Mallika was still snoring. No one seemed to want to budge from their seats. She looked out of the window and caught sight of a woman standing on the other side of the road. She was shouting something in Marathi. She was saying, 'Get out and stop the men, they will kill him. No man can save him.'

Mallika opened the door and jumped out. The shouting and screaming of the men was unbearable, almost bestial by now. Three men kicked the driver, who was crouching on the ground and using his arms to shield his head. One man grabbed him by the arm and, pulling him up, punched the side of his head with his fist before dropping him to the ground. The other men continued to kick him relentlessly. The crowd of people wanting to hit the driver seemed to be growing. Mallika began to understand what the woman across the road meant as another man pulled the driver up and raised his fist to hit him. She grasped the man's wrist and shouted, 'Stop, stop, stop, stop you all!'

And instantly, they stopped and turned to face her. She released the man's hand.

He looked at her, startled out of his frenzy, as she shouted, 'It was an accident. You have beaten him so much; do you want to kill him? Let him go now, let him go.'

The autorickshaw driver came forward, 'My rickshaw is damaged. Who will pay to fix it?'

'Here, take this,' said a man. Mallika turned to look.

It was her snoring neighbour from the jeep. He held out a hundred-rupee note to the rickshaw driver.

'This is not enough.'

The man gave him another hundred rupees. 'This is all I can give.'

Before any further talk, at the sound of ignition, the man pulled Mallika by the arm and said, 'Come on, brave woman, let's get back into the jeep before the crowd stirs again.'

They rushed back into the jeep and swiftly pulled away as the driver wiped blood from his face with a handkerchief.

20

THE CROSS-COUNTRY PLAN

Sriram had left home much later than usual that morning. Mallika had not yet returned from vaari and he didn't want to dwell on that as work was piling up in her absence. So he was pleasantly surprised to see her.

Mallika was startled to see Sriram striding into the office just before noon, looking haggard in a dishevelled shirt, scruffy beard, and just a terse remark instead of his usual cheerful greeting.

'So you're back.'

'Yes, Sriram. But what's happened to you?'

'I was sick for nearly a week, viral fever. Better now.'

He walked into his room. She followed behind, hoping to continue the conversation.

'For some reason, I didn't feel the need to go right till the end and so I decided to return four days early,' Mallika felt the need to explain.

'What...what reason? What do you mean, early?'

'It was...oh...we can talk about it some other time. What about the plans for the padayatra?'

Mallika watched him rub his eyes with his knuckles. He leaned back in the chair, closing his eyes.

'Sriram, is something wrong? What is the matter?'

'I haven't contacted anyone for the padayatra while you were gone. I couldn't. You will have to work on it now. We have lost two weeks.'

'Alright, Sriram. I'll get—'

'You were gone for too long. Don't tell me you think you are back early.'

Mallika sat facing him, elbows on the table, a little bewildered at his accusatory tone and what seemed like a resentment and perhaps disapproval.

'You know,' she offered, 'I thought of you when I saw a group of doctors volunteering on the vaari. They were...'

But Sriram looked on in stony silence, forcing her to mumble, 'Ah...okay, I think I'll get started on work.'

Back at her desk, Mallika's thoughts drifted back to her journey, trying to assimilate all that had happened over the last two weeks. One thing that stood out was the hypocrisy of the political system and an administration that honoured and felicitated farmers as pilgrims on the vaari. But the same farmers were abused in their role as food providers for the nation. She could not wait to discuss this with Sriram. But that could come later. She was happy that she had made the decision to return early. She didn't know what to make of Sriram accusing her of having been away for too long. He had agreed to her going and she had gone only after seeking his permission. Then what was it that troubled him?

She gave up trying to guess and decided to ring Trevor and Seema, fixing to meet them in the evening to discuss a tentative plan for the padayatra. They would need more volunteers and a larger team to undertake this ambitious journey. It was not going to be restricted to Maharashtra but spread across the country, through nine states. She had yet to share this new idea with Sriram. She tiptoed back to his room and found him resting on the desk, his folded arms cradling his face. She felt a little worried about him; he should be resting at home. Perhaps the fever had put him in a bad mood. She stepped out for lunch and on returning found a note from Sriram saying he had left for the day.

'Grumpy,' she whispered aloud.

The next morning, Sriram looked like a new man. The overgrown beard, well-trimmed. He seemed himself again, cheerful and distant at the same time. Feeling encouraged, she told him of her idea.

'Traversing through nine states? Are you crazy? We can't afford to take such an extensive journey at this stage. We had an overall plan for Maharashtra, let's stick to that.'

'Sriram, we must make it a bigger journey, a long march. There are several, even poorer and more backward districts in these states that I have listed. We should visit them. Instead of walking everywhere, if we use a combination of transport—trains and buses—and walk for some parts, it won't be impossible.'

'And how did you decide on these districts?'

'I told you it came up when we were discussing with Bhaskar Prabhu during our Vidarbha visit.'

'Mallika, let me think about it before we finalize anything,' responded Sriram tersely.

Perhaps she was right. Instead of travelling through and exploring just one state, it would be better to spread the study across more regions, at least as many as humanly possible. And she was certainly right about one thing. There was no point in walking everywhere. He liked her sincerity and practical outlook, though he did not mention this to her.

The next day, Sriram told Mallika to make a padayatra plan across the country instead of only Maharashtra. She was happy but he continued to be very worried about it. He was not sure if he had taken the right decision.

Nevertheless, Sriram and Mallika selected ten volunteers from twenty-three young men and women who had responded to advertisements in college campuses and in a few newspapers. Mallika also asked Swati—who had just quit her job after a big argument with her boss—to join them if she wished to. Swati jumped at the chance of travelling all over the country with a team of volunteers. This meant that an additional—and more importantly, an objective— person would be making notes of their journey from which real statistics could be compiled. She also contacted Vikram Sonare in Wardha. He too agreed to join them.

The preparations for the journey took nearly two months. Mallika, Vikram, Trevor and Seema decided on the route, made train reservations for the group, and figured out the interim bus journeys on state transport or private buses. The tickets for these were to be booked as the journey progressed.

21

A LONG JOURNEY

The journey began on the twelfth of September as Mallika, Sriram, Trevor, Seema, Swati and the ten volunteers left on a train from Mumbai CST to Akola city in Vidarbha. Vikram travelled from Wardha to join them there. Due to insufficient rains the previous year and delayed monsoons that year, Akola, also known as 'Cotton City', was facing an acute water shortage. They took a state transport bus to reach Barasgaon village in Akola district.

Six volunteers spread out to visit as many houses in the village in order to talk to the people, discuss their problems and record the conversations. They also invited the villagers to join the rest of their group at a small, open ground where they had assembled, right in the centre of the village. Five hundred was the recorded population of Barasgaon. But only about a hundred-odd villagers lived there.

Mallika, Sriram and Vikram walked up to a woman whose head of white hair was loosely draped over by a bluish-green sari. As they got closer to her hut, a man coughed, walked up to the door and spat out. A mynah landed on the thatched roof of the hut, ruffled and pecked at its brown feathers and, raising its yellow beak in the air, flew away. The man, in loose pyjama bottoms and a thin cotton tunic, stood next to his wife. The woman gestured to the strangers, offering a cot that lay outside the house to sit, while the couple squatted on the floor at the entrance. Sriram and the others settled themselves on the cot and then a few more volunteers walked up and sat on the ground, facing the old couple. Sriram folded his hands in greeting, 'Namaskar. How are you doing?'

'Alright,' said the old woman. Her name was Shashitai, and the tiredness showed on her face, and her forehead was pinched in distress. A young girl came running out and sat on her lap. Shashitai opened up. 'This is Sarika, my granddaughter. She is two years old now. I am taking care of her.'

'Where are her parents?'

'My son and daughter-in-law are in Gujarat.'

'Gujarat?'

'Yes. They have gone there for work. They will return after the rains come.' She looked up to the sky as if in prayer.

'Why did they have to go all the way to Gujarat for work?'

'What to do? There is no work here or in the nearby villages. We have hardly any money. He is old now,' she said, looking at her husband, 'and always sick. He cannot work. I can manage the house and take care of this girl. That is all we can do now.'

'Do you have only one son?'

'I have a daughter. She is married and lives in a different village. Her family is also preoccupied with their problems. I had one more son. He killed himself.'

Sriram saw the girl and looked away. Mallika wrote in her notebook. One volunteer cleared his throat. Two stood up and shuffled their feet. Vikram, watching the old man, moved to help him as he began to cough and shake uncontrollably. He rose unsteadily and went inside, holding on to Vikram's shoulder.

'Is he sick?' Sriram asked Shashitai, looking towards her husband. 'Have you taken him to a doctor?'

'Yes, once. He has asthma. Last year he had typhoid. He picks up infections easily. But what can we do?'

'You must take him to the district hospital. You have a young child at home. She should not catch an infection.'

Shashitai let out a long sigh and as she ran her hand over the girl's head and caressed her cheek. 'What has to happen will happen. Even to this child.'

Mallika moved closer and rested her palm on the girl's forehead. It was warm. 'Have you taken her to a dispensary? Is she taking any medicine for her fever?'

'No, no. Which dispensary are you talking about? There is no doctor in this village and no dispensary. The nearest one is miles and miles away. Who is going to take her there? She will be well again, in a few days' time.'

Sriram opened his black bag, pulled out his stethoscope and examined the girl first and then her grandfather. He gave a bottle of medicine for the girl and a small packet of pills for the man. Mallika looked on, thinking how random and inadequate the prescriptions were. How much could a drop of water go in quenching chronic thirst?

Swati wrote furiously in her notebook:

There must be many more children like Sarika. Children who are sick, in need of a doctor's attention, but the

only option they have is to wait and heal on their own
or else succumb to their maladies. There is simply no
access to doctors and hospitals. These children are meant
to be part of the generation that will make our country
a superpower. Can they do that by living this way? Will
children like Sarika be able to compete with children from
well-off families in urban India? How would they even
begin to compete with children from other developed
countries? The questions are baffling and we are all left
speechless. I feel helpless.

As they walked away, Mallika wondered what that girl would
be like in a few more years. She found the answer when
they met another young girl standing outside the next house.

Mallika went to her and, taking her hands, said, 'My
name is Mallika. What is your name?'

'Asha.'

'Do you go to school?'

'No.'

'How old are you?'

The girl said nothing more and ran inside. Her
grandfather, sprawled out on a cot outside, sat up. Two
younger boys were playing in the mud at the side of the
house.

'Who else is in your family?' Vikram asked the man.

'Only four of us now. The girl takes care of us. Their
parents have gone to the city to look for construction work.'

Swati continued to write:

These children, the future citizens of the country,
what kind of childhood do they have? All we can do is
watch, listen, ask questions and take notes. What else
can we do?

The next leg of the journey was to go northwards. They first made their way back to Akola Junction, spending the night at a lodge near the railway station. In the morning, they caught the Gondwana Express taking them on an eleven-hour journey to Hoshangabad in Madhya Pradesh. During the ride, Sriram and Mallika quietly read through the notes made by Swati and two other volunteers. They read each others' notes as well.

It was Seema who broke the silence.

'What are the reasons for the hardships of the villagers we met in Akola?'

'The answer lies in several factors,' said Mallika. 'They have small land holdings. There is no water available for irrigation. They are completely dependent on rains. Even if they manage to sell their crop, the money will only last for a few months. They need more money. There is no money to dig wells or use water pumps.'

'Can't they get loans from nationalized banks?'

'Most of them try to take loans. Often their previous loans have not been repaid, which makes it all the more difficult for the next loan to be sanctioned.'

'So they just have to wait for the next good crop?'

'There is no certainty that the rains will oblige and give them a good crop. The prices of seeds, fertilizers and pesticides are rising constantly, making the cost of growing crops more expensive. If they go to the private moneylenders, they charge exorbitant interest rates. So the only way out is to migrate to another place to find work.'

'But they must be making some money as labourers elsewhere.'

'Yes, they must be making some money. But, Seema,

you have to understand that all the money they earn is needed to buy food. For other essentials, like clothes and medicines, they have very little or sometimes even no money left. Definitely none to celebrate festivals, which is perhaps, the only time of the year when they can derive some pleasure in their lives.'

'They just manage to eat and live. They are just about able to survive,' added Mallika.

Trevor, who was listening intently to all this, declared: 'Did you know that a law was enacted in the state of Maharashtra to assure a job to each and every person so that there would be no need to migrate for work? It is supposed to have some connection to the Professional Tax that employees throughout Maharashtra pay, but I don't know exactly what it is.'

Sriram explained: 'In 1972, there was a severe famine throughout rural Maharashtra. People from villages began migrating to urban areas. They started living in the growing slums of Mumbai and other cities. To deal with the situation, the Right to Employment Law was passed so that all men and women in rural areas would get work, which the state government was supposed to provide. But the government had no money to fund the employment programmes. So they introduced a new "Professional Tax" that every employee in Maharashtra pays, whether in the public or private sector. It is deducted by the employer. But has the money generated by this tax created jobs in villages? It is there for all of us to see.'

Noticing the morose faces of the entire group, he quickly added, 'But the next district we are visiting, Hoshangabad, is known to be very prosperous. So we will get to see some happy villagers and they may even offer us a rustic feast.'

This was not enough to cheer them up, however, so Mallika suggested they play antakshari. The group was divided into two teams. Finding Vikram missing, Trevor left his seat to look for him and the two young men returned a few minutes later.

'Vikram, where did you disappear? Come, come, we are playing antakshari and I am sure you know a lot of songs. You are in my team and we have to defeat Mallika's. But where were you?' asked Sriram.

'I was standing at the door.'

'What were you doing there?'

'Dreaming!'

That snapped the sombre mood and everyone laughed before breaking into a boisterous singing competition.

At six-thirty that evening, they reached Hoshangabad city on the southern bank of the Narmada. They walked from the station to an inexpensive lodging house on Station Road. Vikram, Trevor and two other young men went out to make travel arrangements for the next day. The next morning at around six, they walked to the bus depot to board the state transport bus for Fasalpur, which was a two-hour journey.

An unexpected silence greeted the group when they reached Fasalpur village. A farmer, considered fairly prosperous just three years ago, had been found burnt to death that same morning. The local police recorded it as a possible accident. But a retired Professor who knew the dead man told them a different story.

'He was a very smart farmer. When there was a demand

for soybeans, he was the first to start cultivating the crop. Yields were very high in the beginning. But after three years, it dropped off so much that costs could not be recovered. To make matters worse, the market price of soybeans spiralled down as a result of the international trade agreements. The man had to resort to taking loans, and when he could not repay them last year, he was completely devastated.'

The dejected group then wangled free rides on three bullock-carts heading to the nearby village of Choksar, where a different kind of activity was going on. A man, Kewal Singh, had built a toilet in his house with help from his neighbours and other men in the village. It was the first and only toilet in the village. When the volunteers arrived, everyone was waiting expectantly out in the road.

'Who are you waiting for?' asked Swati. 'Are you expecting some government official?'

Some of the men laughed at the question and after much teasing and cajoling from the men, Kewal Singh replied, 'No, no, not any government official. My wife refused to stay with me because there was no toilet in my house. She went back to her mother's place. So with the help of my friends, I built this toilet. She is going to return today. We are waiting for her.'

After an hour, the wife reached the village along with her brother. The villagers insisted that the bride and groom exchange garlands, and there was loud cheering and applause when they did. Other women looked at the rebel bride in admiration.

Mallika, Swati and Seema went on to talk to the other women. They returned to tell the rest of the group that the women had already started strategizing to convince their husbands to build toilets. They had decided to nominate the rebel bride for the next panchayat elections and make her the sarpanch. As chief of the village council, she would support them in their demand.

In every village that the group visited, Vikram Sonare disappeared to mingle with as many villagers as he could, while Sriram and the others talked to a few of the men and women. On the train journey from Hoshangabad further north to Uttar Pradesh, Sriram joined him at his favourite spot, the door.

'Vikram, I notice that you keep disappearing while the rest of us talk to people. Would you like to share what you have been doing?'

'Of course, Sriram sir. I am trying to connect with as many people as I can. I am taking their names, addresses and mobile numbers. I am also asking them about other people in other villages and taking their names and phone numbers as well.'

'Why are you doing all this?'

'It is my dream, sir, an idea. Just now, I am only keeping all the information ready to build a network. There is so much more to do yet.'

'A network? For what?'

'Sir, I will use it when the time comes.'

'When the time comes for what, Vikram?'

'I don't know what exactly yet. I don't know what to call it. But when I know it, I will tell Mallika, and of course, you too.'

In Chilgaon village located in Banda district of Uttar Pradesh, Vikram spotted a man deeply engrossed in some calculations on several sheets of paper while numerous men

waited in a queue to be paid for their work through the
Rural Job Scheme. One man approached the number-jotting
supervisor and, pressing his thumb on an ink pad, dabbed
an impression against fifteen names. The man accepted
money due for fifteen workers from the supervisor and
walked away nonchalantly. Other men in the queue watched
the proceedings in silence, while patiently waiting for their
turn for the daily wages. Some of the men were forced to
return home, wages unpaid, even after hours of waiting in
the hot sun.

The young volunteers in the group were shocked to
witness this open daylight robbery but the villagers remained
unmoved.

One man told Vikram, 'You see, we all know what goes
on here everyday. Every child in the village knows that the
Rural Job Schemes are a new venture for officials and their
cronies to make money. Those of us who are lucky, manage
to get some scraps from what is left.'

While passing through another town soon thereafter, a
man accompanying them pointed out, 'Look! Look there.
That is the "Job Scheme Colony".'

'Job Scheme Colony?'

'Yes, those are the houses built by officials and
contractors from the money pilfered off the Rural Job
Scheme. You will find such houses in district after district.
Don't look so shocked!'

Amid the poverty and the lack of basic facilities they
encountered, the group also met some exceptionally
enterprising people. Thirty-year-old Dattaram had left his
village in Banda district and come to the city of Kanpur
looking for work. After working on several odd jobs as a

labourer, a waiter and an errand-man, an idea struck him as he was shining his employer's shoes one morning. He got hold of two street boys wandering near the railway station and started a shoe-polishing business. While the two boys polished shoes, he rallied more customers by talking to railway passengers and passers-by. He then set up a small shoe-repair shop. Within a year's time he had started to make shoes and sell them at very cheap prices. 'There is always a market for cheap goods of good quality and my shoes were soon in demand,' said Dattaram. 'Now I have a big order from a prominent shoe shop and another one for shoes for schoolboys from a large residential school near Lucknow.'

In Kosipur village in Bihar, the river flowing through the village, which was the main source of water and was once well known for its clear waters, was now dark and dirty. Its surroundings reeked with the stench of untreated sewage flowing in from the nearby city of Patna. The villagers had no option but to drill tube wells, which were also contaminated with the river water. The pipeline carrying drinking water was about 6 kilometres away. Every morning, women and girls walked the long distance to fill pots of water and carry them back.

The group fell silent that afternoon as they ate their meal at a roadside dhaba and boarded a train to Ranchi in Jharkhand. A few of the volunteers had taken a different train to return to Mumbai, leaving just eight in the group now. All of them were weary and ready for sleep when they reached the guesthouse late that evening. As Seema and Swati drifted off to sleep, Mallika glanced out of the second-floor window of their room at the dimly lit street below. She spotted a figure receding to the far end and knew it was Sriram. An hour later, she peered out again to find Sriram still there pacing up and down, lost in his thoughts.

By planning a journey much bigger than Sriram had intended, Mallika had pushed him to the edge. He had already started thinking that this elaborate journey had probably been a mistake. They had attempted to do much more than what they were capable of. Sriram's thoughts harked back to the early days of starting his free clinic in Mumbai. How simple and straightforward his work had been. If only he could replicate that in just one village, he would be happy.

Mallika wondered if she should go out and ask Sriram what was bothering him. At just that moment, Sriram turned around and came back into the guesthouse.

Next morning they travelled by bus to the Simdega district, alighting at Nahuripur village. A short walk away from the bus stop was a school from which they heard loud cheering as they drew nearer. A girls' hockey match was in full swing. The hockey sticks were improvised from bamboo poles, bent at one end. The group joined the crowd of villagers and watched the game, which finished 7-4. A while later, their coach gathered all the girls from both teams in a circle and they all shouted together in jubilation, raising their hands in air: 'Hip, hip, hooray! Hip hip hooray!'

As they all sang, one of the schoolteachers handed out motichur laddoos to all the children present. Mallika asked the players if they would like to play hockey professionally; a few smiled shyly and some even rolled their eyes. One girl came forward.

'Yes, I want to play, but going to Ranchi for training

requires money. My parents don't have so much to spend. But I want to go.'

'I want to play for India,' said another girl. The others who had been silently listening started to open up.

'Yes, we all want to play. Like in *Chak De India*!'

The group stayed the night in the village. That night Mallika fell ill. It was just a slight fever, she told Swati, but when Sriram heard of it he insisted on examining her. They were all sleeping out in the open, on cots provided by the villagers, the three women at one end and all the men at the other in a row. Sriram brought out his stethoscope to examine her, making Mallika feel like a patient. He disappeared for a while and returned, saying, 'Mallika, I think you should go and sleep in one of those houses there. I have spoken to the people and they will accommodate you.'

'No, Sriram, I'm alright here.'

'I'm the doctor here and you have to listen. Now, please.'

Sriram instructed Seema and Swati to go with her. Mallika picked up her rucksack but Sriram quickly snatched it from her as they walked towards the house. The woman living there gathered up her bedcovers and walked to her sister's house next door. Mallika thought about how this would never happen in a city. She spread out her tired body on the cot in the front room while Seema and Swati slept on mats on the kitchen floor.

Throughout the night, Sriram kept a check on Mallika's fever while she slept.

On one such occasion while monitoring her fever, he took her hand and turned it in his own, tempted to interweave his fingers with hers. He wanted to soothe her weary face and parched lips. Releasing her hand and gently placing it by her side, he picked up the handkerchief now drying on her forehead and dipped it in the bowl of water and eau de cologne. He had been marvelling at her, and the general efficiency of women, when she had given him the tiny bottle of cologne from her bag earlier. They did not have it in the two first-aid kits they were carrying. The idea of starting a free clinic in a village returned to him and he thought Mallika would be a perfect partner. She would help him in organizing it and spreading it to more villages. He was surprised to find himself thinking of her as an equal rather than his subordinate.

Squeezing out the excess water into the bowl, he unfolded the white handkerchief and placed it gently on her forehead.

Mallika gazed at Sriram through half-open lids. She ran her tongue over her lips, feeling their papery dryness. She was feverish. Sriram picked up a glass of water and helped her to sit up partially. With his arm around her shoulders, he cradled her while she drank thirstily, even as the thin edge of the wide brass tumbler hurt the corners of her lips. Whispering thanks, she fell asleep again. He watched her until it was time for him to sleep, and walked out to his bed under the starry sky.

The next morning, with all traces of fever gone, Mallika woke up, rested and refreshed.

'How are you feeling?' asked Sriram as they gathered around a tree and drank tea before resuming their journey.

'Much better. I'm fine, in fact.'

That afternoon when they finished eating lunch, Sriram touched her forehead and then her wrist to check for any fever.

'What's the verdict, doctor?' asked Mallika.

'The fever is gone...I think you are ready for the next leg of our journey to Orissa.'

The state of Odisha had been in the news constantly because of the powerful protests the farmers there had conducted in their fight against the steel giant, Provok. When the group reached Haripur village, there was a very heavy police bandobast.

'There are hundreds of policemen here. Why?' asked Mallika.

Vikram was the first to figure it out. 'Look, behind the police barricades, there's a huge crowd of men, women and children. They have formed a human wall...look.'

Vikram walked as close as he could, fascinated by the will of these people. There were so many women in that human wall. He walked around the gathering and moved closer to the protesters, hoping to talk to the locals. Although some of the villagers had agreed to give up their land to the government, many others were unwilling to let go of their livelihood.

A leader of the betel leaf farmers told Vikram in Hindi, 'We have been growing these leaves for generations now. We earn well, more than what the government pays in their job schemes. Why should we give up working on our own land and work for an outside company? How long will they stay here? They will exploit the land and extract iron ore from the mines...but for how long? Ten, twenty, thirty years? When they have filled their pockets they will leave, closing down the mines and factories behind them. And what will happen to us? There is no guarantee in all this. We will not give up the land that our ancestors have nurtured for years, that we are nurturing now. Why should we give up being our own masters and become slaves of a steel company? Just because the government wants us to do it?'

Vikram felt inspired by this man and the determination the villagers had displayed. He then decided to leave the group and travel to Kolkata. 'I am meeting a friend from Meghalaya,' he explained. 'His name is Livingston Das and he will take me to Shillong. He has started a computer training centre for poor schoolchildren and college students there. The schoolchildren learn for free but the college students pay him back by taking up basic data-entry work for his web content business. Some of the college students have now joined him and his business is growing every year.'

'What will you do there?' asked Mallika.

'Learn from him. I also hope to pay him back for the amount he contributed towards my travel expenses. He is very kind and like a brother to me. There is a lot that I want to learn about computers, the internet, phones and other technical things. It will help me in carrying out my plans. I will tell you about it all very soon.'

The rest of them took a train to Hyderabad and stayed in the city for the night. In the morning they boarded a bus to Mahbubnagar district to go to the Kulucherla village. None of the families there made enough to sustain themselves from their primary occupation of farming. Except for a few, all of them worked as manual labourers in the government programmes for digging canals, wells and building roads.

A middle-aged farmer named Prashant Reddy told Sriram, 'But this government programme employs us for less than half a year. As every adult in the family joins, the number of days of work for each one is reduced. Now even small shopkeepers are working on the programme. With prices constantly rising, nobody is buying much from the shops anyway.'

Another man joined in: 'Delayed rains have ruined our chances of reaping a good crop of the groundnuts that we grow here.'

'How long is the crop cycle?' asked Sriram.

'We sow in June or July and harvest in October and November. Not much time is left for growing another crop. Life has become very difficult for us. Many are leaving to work as labourers in the city. I am also considering it, but I don't know how it will be...'

At the Mahbubnagar bus depot, Sriram talked to a group of seven Adivasi men.

'Where are you going?

'Mumbai,' answered one of them.

'What time is your bus to Mumbai?'

'We will take the next available bus. Ten years ago we would have waited for a whole week for just one bus service to Mumbai. Now there are many, thirty or forty each week.'

'So many?'

'Yes, we have nothing here to live on. We can only go to Mumbai. We will find work there. Some people also go to Pune. I have never been there.' He thumped a palm on his chest, 'For me, only Mumbai.'

'What work will you do there?'

'What work...like building construction work or road digging. What else? We can only do manual work.'

Another man grinned, 'They are always digging and digging roads in the city. That gives us enough work.'

The others laughed.

Sriram bid goodbye to the men as they left for Mumbai. Then the group took another bus to the neighbouring state of Karnataka. Mallika read *The Nation's Voice* and pointed out an article to Sriram:

> A backward caste woman has put up her daughters, aged six and four, for sale. Her husband died two years earlier and she has applied for a job as an anganwadi worker. She passed her matriculation with a first class with distinction and is now eligible to work in the child care centre in Chitradurga district. But other applicants who have only scraped through their matriculation are getting preference. They have the money to bribe officials. Therefore, as a mark of protest, she has put her daughters up for sale, to raise money for a bribe. For two days she has been carrying a large cardboard sign advertising her children for sale and protesting outside the Deputy Commissioner's office, stationing herself and her two daughters there from morning till evening.

In the village of Mannapur in the Belgaum District of Karnataka was a young farmer named Mayuresh. His father had lost all his land to relatives in a property dispute. When the group visited the village, they met him. His father had died two years ago, just after Mayuresh had completed his degree in agriculture science. Unwilling to fight with relatives, Mayuresh had enrolled for a research programme at the university to work on organic cultivation of herbs.

'I bought a small piece of land, only half an acre, and started cultivating herbs. I was able to sell my produce to Ayurvedic medicine practitioners. Simply by word of mouth, my business grew.'

'How much land do you have now?'

'Oh, one of the relatives sold his land to me at a cheap price. Now I have three acres, and six people are working on my farm. I also grow some fruits. The business will prosper if I work hard. But that is not enough for me now. I am also teaching other farmers about organic cultivation. Seeing my success, some farmers' children in my village and nearby villages are also now interested in earning an agricultural science degree, and they want to work on their farms instead of going to the city to look for jobs.'

From Belgaum, the group boarded a train to return to Mumbai, bringing their long journey to an end. But Mallika felt their real work had only just begun. While she constantly discussed the journey with Sriram on the train ride, he toyed with the idea of free clinics in villages. He would break it to Mallika at the first opportunity after their return. The others in their group mostly listened or dozed off from sheer exhaustion.

22

THE NEW CO-OPERATIVE

Vikram had learned a great deal from his friend Livingston Das. Livingston had also helped Vikram build a database of the contacts he had made during his recent journey. He had decided to continue adding names to it in the future as he spread the network further. A deeper understanding of social media and mobile phones had led him to think about using technology to create a network of people, who would help initiate the movement he had in mind. It was only a germ of an idea, but after learning everything that he did from Livingston, he was more confident of taking it forward. When he left Shillong, his friend promised to visit him in Sonsawali someday.

'That day should not be too far from now, my friend,' said Vikram, as they hugged and said goodbye. Vikram thanked him again for the old laptop he had received as a gift. Das said graciously, 'It is my little contribution to your cause.' Only Vikram knew how invaluable his real contribution was.

On his return journey, Vikram made a couple of unplanned stops, meeting more people and adding more information to the database. He met a young architect in Delhi who wanted to quit his job designing luxury hotels and build a model village. The architect also introduced Vikram to a group of small farmers from Punjab who were interested in the plans for the model village.

In the village of Chandaur in the Mirpur district of Uttar Pradesh, Vikram met Razia and her family. Razia Patel was the sole breadwinner in a family of four sisters and two brothers. Her elderly father was disabled and her mother had died recently. Razia had a knack for stitching and designing clothes for weddings and festive occasions that were much admired by the village women. She had set up her own shop and her brothers sold the merchandise in other villages close to Chandaur. The business had grown so much that she had managed to employ seven other young women and three men in her village. Other women interested in the trade came to her for training, which she willingly imparted.

Vikram returned to Sonsawali brimming with enthusiasm. He first went back to his only solace from the cruel world—the anthill. As he watched the furious activity of the ants, a plan started to take shape in his mind.

Vikram decided to kickstart a new co-operative movement. During his recent travels through the country, while the poverty and hardships of people had stared him in the face, his mind kept going back to his own emerging philosophy of life. It demanded that in order to eradicate poverty, a person has to be part of a co-operative that works on the principle of shared work and income. It had developed into a full-fledged strategy in his mind and he was eager to share it with his friends. All the people he had met were to be the starting points of the network that Vikram was building. Each one would be a focal point, and was to help widen the network within their immediate community and nearby areas.

Nothing seemed impossible now.

When Vikram woke the next morning, he decided to talk to his friends and other young men in his village, especially those he knew would listen to him. A dozen of them gathered around him. Many were curious to know where he had been for the last few weeks. Vikram was selective in what he told them about his journey, about some of the people he had met. Everyone was listening to him with rapt attention. When he finished, there was a long silence.

Then Vikram's friend Mohan asked, 'So, what now? Why are you telling us all this?'

Vikram looked at them all, turning a pebble in his hand.

'I went on this journey with several other people, most of them were young people like us. They were social workers and student volunteers from Mumbai and some from smaller towns. They were trying to understand the poverty and hardships of people like us, living in villages. But who knows these things better than you and I? We are born into this world of never-ending hardships. I often feel our lives offer us little prospects for making things better. I met so many people across the country, people who also feel the way we feel. The same problems: relentless hard work, work, work, work and nothing much to show in return. But not everyone accepts this quietly, like we do. There are villages where people are fighting against the government and the powerful industrialists. They are fighting to keep their land from being given away or sold off at cheap prices to these bigwigs. People are putting their lives in jeopardy, not just men but women and children too. They are putting up a brave fight. I saw two hundred people daring to rise up against a thousand-strong police force that had the backing of money and power. Those people are not afraid to fight. Not afraid to lose their lives or get injured. They are so passionate about working on lands they own. I saw groups of tribal people fighting to keep a mountain from being mined by a corporation for its own profits. They are doing that only because the mountain is important to their lives, it is sacred to them. It has been so for generations They are not giving up. Why should we give up our lands and our way of life?'

'What do you mean, Vikram? What exactly are you saying?'

'You see, I used to think that we are all resigned to our fates here in the village. I know we are not indifferent, but we are not doing anything about it either. I know most of us dream of living in a proper house and having enough money for our family, of sending our children to proper schools, and having good doctors and hospitals to rely on when we fall ill. We also want good roads and better facilities for our community. But I want all of us to think about what we really want. Should we go to the cities and work as labourers? Subsist on odd jobs and live in slums? Or do we want to make real progress and have a truly better life? If those who are in power cannot give us what we want on our terms, then I say that we should seize power from the hands of the powerful.'

Mohan laughed and a few others joined in. But the rest remained serious and thoughtful.

Soham, the quietest and youngest in the group, asked, 'Exactly what do you want us to do? Kill the politicians and the officials?'

Those who had laughed earlier, now looked nervously at Vikram. They were startled when Vikram laughed.

'No, not kill the officials or the politicians. But enter politics ourselves.'

Mohan spoke up again. 'Which party do you want to join? They are ultimately all the same, bloody betrayers. They promise the mountain at election time and after they are elected, they don't give us even a handful of grains.'

'Yeah, which party? Which party should we join?'

'A new party,' Vikram said.

They all became quiet and waited for him to continue.

'We will form a new political party. But before that, we have to form a new co-operative of people from villages as well as cities. What we need is a co-operative that ties several villages to one or more towns and cities in a sort of business of exchanging goods and services.'

Vikram and his friends talked about their plans from morning till late in the night. They ate their meals together so they wouldn't have to break the spontaneous rush of ideas for the new life that they were about to begin.

—

Meanwhile in Mumbai, Sriram read through Mallika's report of their long journey. He was anxious to tell her about his new plans. Before the journey, whatever he had in mind seemed simple. But now it was all too overwhelming. He was also completely distracted by the letter he had received from Dhanraj Industries. They had invited him to talk about his work in the social sector. They wanted to involve him in their Corporate Social Responsibility initiative. It took him a while to go through the report and face his dilemma. Should he work to set up free clinics in villages as he had wanted to, or should he explore this seemingly attractive alternative? He would have liked to talk to Mallika, but decided against it.

'So, Mallika, what do you think our next steps should be?'

'I think the entire countryside and our villages require so much to be done by the government. Communities must have all basic infrastructure and amenities in place. But most importantly, what has to absolutely stop is this looting of resources meant for the development of rural areas by the nexus of politicians, bureaucrats, contractors, businessmen.'

'Oh, that's quite a bold proposition. How can that be done?'

'All the citizens, particularly the ordinary people, should participate in political processes.'

'That is already happening. We all vote. We are a democracy.'

'No, that is a kind of passive involvement. We should play a more active role. More people should stand for elections.'

Sriram laughed. 'That's interesting. You mean as independent candidates?'

'Yes, er...no...I mean the people should form a new political party. Bring in fresh blood to challenge the current political system.'

'That is indeed a great idea, but much, much easier said than done. Do you know how many political parties already exist in India? Can you even begin to fathom the effort involved in doing what you are suggesting?'

Mallika grabbed the armrests of her chair and almost got up, 'Are you saying it can't happen?'

'No. Nothing is impossible. Anything can happen. So who are the villains you are fighting against?'

'We are fighting against ignorance and illiteracy. We will have to fight against corruption, which I really don't know how to tackle. And most importantly, we must fight against discrimination. This last one will be the most challenging. I envision a time in the near future where any Indian can walk as the social and political equal of another, no matter what his or her profession, occupation, economic status, religion, caste or gender. I imagine a cultural centre in every village, town or city where people could gather, and sit and talk to each other over a cup of tea or a glass of wine. Can you imagine such a situation? Can you think how great the intellectual maturity of our people would be to reach such a state as that? It will take years, decades, but we have to begin somewhere, sometime.'

Sriram wanted to laugh again but refrained.

'Mallika, I must say here that you are getting quite carried away. I mean, do you want to work in the villages to improve conditions there and help make the lives of the people better? I'm asking because first you said you wanted to start a new political party that is grounded in the here and now. And then you talked of a society, a transformation that, er, resembles what? Utopia?'

'Sriram, let's forget the utopia bit for the moment. Maybe it is much too early to think of such things. Maybe it can't happen during our lifetime. But let's look at the other thing. Politicians end up making ten times or more their original wealth when they are in power. That is why they cling to it. And it is a known fact that a majority of elected representatives are much richer than the average Indian. Shouldn't someone do something about it?'

Sriram now laughed heartily, but there was no hint of a smile on Mallika's face. She ignored his attempt to make light of her ideas, though she recognized that he was far more realistic.

'Mallika, you know what it takes to become a politician in India. And yet you are saying that citizens like us should not only get involved in politics but actually form a new political party. How long do you think it will last?'

'Sriram, remember the questions you threw at me when you first interviewed me? Well, I have the answers now. I know what I want to do. It's terrifying to even think about it. But I want to do it. I know that Vikram has already begun to think and act along this track. Or maybe he has been working on this idea for sometime.'

Noting Sriram's silence, Mallika got fidgety. 'Sriram, why are you so silent? What do you think?'

'Mallika, I don't want to be a spoilsport but I am thinking along different lines.'

'Different?'

'I want to start a free clinic in a village and then replicate that model in other villages some years down the line. And I believe your abilities at efficiently organizing are going to be valuable in taking this forward.'

It was Mallika's turn now to go silent.

When Sriram recollected their conversation later that evening, he compared the Mallika of the very first interview with the present one and marvelled at how much she had changed. The timid and docile Mallika was gone and yes, he finally admitted to himself, it was wondrous to watch her talk. How animated, serious, passionate and confident she was while putting forth her ideas, even though he had scoffed at them.

For the next few months, Sriram and Mallika continued with their work in Mumbai as before. Sriram had almost stopped talking about the padayatra and was working on identifying a village where he would start his first clinic. Mallika, feeling a little betrayed by his sudden lack of enthusiasm, spoke to Trevor and Swati. Vikram also came to Mumbai at this time and she had particularly long discussions with him. He told her about the rapid progress he was making in building up his contacts and establishing his network. His friend Livingston Das had visited him in Sonsawali and together, they had set up a programme that could be used to send messages and emails to all the contacts they had collected. However, not everyone had access to email. So the task of contacting people was also carried out by post or telegram, wherever necessary. A number of other people were also identified to be part of a chain of personal messengers in places where all means of communication were absent. Mallika told Vikram about Sriram's growing disinterest in their new political movement.

'Oh, but why?'

'He wants to start a free clinic in a village and then replicate that in other villages. '

'Well, during the time we spent travelling together, I had many opportunities to observe him and get to know him. I think he may not like to do something so radical.'

'Vikram, you seem to be sure about this.'

'Well, he is also much older than us,' Vikram laughed.

'I know, you mean older and wiser. Are we being foolish?'

'No, Mallika. Well, maybe a little. But there is always a bit of foolishness in idealism, isn't there?'

They were both silent and thoughtful. Vikram then asked her very seriously.

'Mallika, tell me if you are or aren't committed to our movement?'

'Of course I am!'

'What if Sriram tells you not to get involved in this movement because after all, you are his employee.'

'He can't do that. I will do what I want to.'

'Good, I'm glad to hear that Mallika. But don't get into an argument with him about this. He is very knowledgeable and if he does start free clinics in many villages, that can be useful for us at some point. His idea is equally important and innovative. Now I must go meet Trevor.'

Trevor had taken up an assignment with a market research firm to conduct a lifestyle survey. For this, he had confirmed appointments with members of elite clubs in Mumbai, and had to visit the members in their homes. Vikram accompanied him, posing as his assistant, and was amazed by the sheer size of the tall buildings in which they lived. What stunned him even more was the opulence of many of the homes they went to.

'These are some kind of modern palaces,' he said to Trevor after leaving one of the houses. 'But in the light of those high, sparkling chandeliers, I see the dark insides of village homes, lit by candles or petromax or a single bulb. In their elegant china tea sets, I see women from our countryside bent over blackened cooking pots in smoking heat and fire. In their large living rooms with cool marble floors and luxurious sofas, I see workers and labourers after a long day at work, sleeping in their dingy slum shanties...'

Over the next six months, Vikram created the network completely, with each contact in his immediate circle linked to sub-circles and so on, making it possible for him to send a message instantly to nearly 80 per cent of all the villages in the country. He was not sure when it would be time to put this network of people into action.

But that year, the food prices kept rising, the monsoon failed to arrive on time, and when it did, the rains were woefully insufficient. There were water shortages everywhere, in the villages and in the cities. Rivers had run dry, many lakes had disappeared and those that were left were shrinking in size, and taps offered barely a trickle of water. Other than the water, the rise in prices of staples like wheat, rice and dal hit the poor the most. Those dependent on the ration shops for their groceries had to wait in ever longer queues, sweltering in the sun, while many of them returned home empty handed because the supply had run out before their turn had even arrived.

There was talk of releasing more foodgrains to the ration shops and distributing it to the poor. In the meantime, television channels showed government godowns filled with undistributed grains that were rotting away, eaten by rats. That led to many panel discussions and shouting matches, while the poor waited patiently for some help from the government.

While they waited, many people starved to death.

The ruling INP claimed that the number of deaths was exaggerated by the media, that there were actually far fewer fatalities. BNP, the opposition party, and other smaller parties raised slogans, both in Parliament and outside it. Every political party held its own protest march to raise their voices against the price rise and lack of food, demanding that the government release more foodgrains to the ration shops. A two-day Bharat Bandh was called by the political parties. During this nationwide strike, all services came to a standstill. The country waited. People in the cities stayed indoors, for there was talk of the possibility of violence. There were power cuts everywhere, even in Mumbai, where the supply had always been regular.

After the two days of bandh were over, things seemed to go back to normal. Opposition parties rejoiced at the success of the strike. They hoped that the government had learnt its lesson. It was reported that the nation had lost a huge amount of revenue due to the stoppage of business and services. The government, on the other hand, was relieved that violence had been averted.

Meanwhile, the famished poor continued to wait patiently, their woes and sorrows drowned in the political din.

Around this time, Mallika met Sudha Bhatkar. She had expected Sudha to talk about the progress in the construction of her new flat. But Sudha appeared rather sad. It turned out that the builder had violated several municipal rules and had been ordered to stop construction. Sudha's money was frozen and the wait for things to get sorted out seemed to be interminable. Mallika told her about the new co-operative movement and Sudha suddenly cheered up.

'Mallika, maybe I should get involved in something like this. Tell me, how can I join?'

'I will tell you when we get together the next time.'

'Okay, but don't forget to call me.'

23

AND THEY MARCH IN

The night before the fateful day, Anita Dhanraj, wife of industrialist Uday Dhanraj, stood on the balcony of her apartment on the twenty-fifth floor and looked at the city below. The diamonds in her rings and earrings sparkled as she took in the twinkling lights of Mumbai. Between clumps of tall buildings lit-up like cylindrical neon torches were pools of darkness. In recent years, these pools of darkness had spread—like ink spreading on blotting paper. These were the city's slums where people, mostly migrants from other parts of the country, were crowded into smaller, shorter, airless shanty homes, breathing in their collective stench.

The alarm rang at six-fifteen the next morning. Anita Dhanraj did not want to be late for her yoga session. Stifling a yawn, her manicured hand with mauve-coloured nails paused mid-air when she heard laughter and realized she was not alone. To her horror, she sat up to find people staring at her. They were squatting all over the Italian marble floor of her bedroom. There were so many of them: twenty or maybe even thirty. She covered her mouth to suppress a loud scream. How did they get into her home?

Most of them were women, and there were children too. Two suckled at their mothers' breasts. A little boy made a peculiar noise as he rubbed glass marbles in his hands. A girl sniffled and the mucous went back up her nostrils, only to leak out again a moment later. Her big, unblinking eyes remained fixed on the fair woman on the bed, as did everyone else's in the room. One of the women tittered and a few more joined in.

As Anita Dhanraj remained calm on the outside, a sense of panic rose within her. She fidgeted with her silky jet-black hair and hugged herself as she wore a silk gown over her skimpy nightie. Her eyes darted to the bedside table, seeking out the leather box that held her jewellery. Just then an old woman walked towards her, hand upheld to reveal three diamond rings on her fingers and a pair of diamond-drop earrings between her lips. Throwing the leather box at her, she pulled out the earrings from between her lips, held them against her cheeks and smiled. Anita Dhanraj let out a long scream. The women just sat and stared, as if nothing unusual was happening.

Where did all these people come from? Anita wondered if she should talk to them to find out. But what were they all doing in her bedroom early in the morning? And where was her husband? What had happened to her retinue of servants? She did not know that most of them had been given a laddoo laced with powdered sleeping pills by the servant in charge. The security guards too had eaten the laddoos with much relish.

She looked for her cell phone, but a girl was playing a game on it while two little boys watched. She looked at the bedroom door. It was shut and two women sat leaning against it. She hugged herself tighter. She dreaded to think what might be on the other side: the husbands of these women? She shuddered at the thought of strange men huddled together outside her room.

As it turned out, she was right. Like the women and children gathered in her bedroom, there were men, women and children all over the city of Mumbai. Sitting and squatting on the streets and the maidans. Traffic throughout the city had come to a halt and the government machinery was busy communicating over telephones.

An idea struck her and she pulled out the drawer of the bedside table. Deep inside rested a small box of her favourite chocolates in golden wrappers. She held out one of them and beckoned the girl playing with her cell phone, 'Chuchuch, chuchuch.'

The girl ran to her, holding her hand forward to pick up the chocolate. Anita closed her palm. The girl understood, returned the cell phone, unwrapped the golden foil of her reward and popped it into her mouth as she toddled away. The two little boys stretched out their hands and received a chocolate each.

Anita pushed the chocolate box back into the drawer and phoned her friend Sumati, the Chief Minister's wife, but she could not get through. Next, she tried her husband Uday's number. That, too, did not work. In a panic, she ran to the door of her bedroom and pushed aside the woman sitting against it. She opened the door and saw that the house was filled with men. All strangers. She closed the door and bolted it. The women in the room continued to stare at her. She switched on the television. When she flicked the remote to a news channel, she felt relieved to be safe in her room, at least for now.

The morning had brought the city of Mumbai, not to mention most of the country, to a standstill. People in their homes watched the news while events played out outside. All along the streets, people were sitting on the roads and the footpaths. Men in white tunics and pyjamas or shirts and trousers stood or sat amongst the crowd. Some men were in dhotis and sported bright turbans or white topis. The women were in saris, their pallus covering their heads or only the shoulders. Many women were in salwar kameez. There were children too, girls in frocks and boys in oversized, soiled T-shirts and shorts, some sitting, many of them standing.

So it had happened. People from rural India had marched into the cities, claiming their rightful place in the nation's prosperity. They wanted a share—a fair share in the better life that their urban countrymen had been enjoying every day of their lives. As the news spread during the course of the day, it became clear that others too had joined the farmers in their protest rally. Other people from the village community, cowherds and shepherds, weavers and blacksmiths, potters and cobblers, had all lent their support, standing firm alongside the farmers. The city folk were not far behind. Slumdwellers showed solidarity too. They only had to walk out of their homes and occupy the streets and maidans situated close to the slums. They entered building compounds and filled up the empty spaces they found. It was a peaceful protest. But as the sheer number of people blocking up the streets and empty grounds rose, fears and rumours of potential violence spread.

How did this come about? Why now? What triggered it?

In a year when the country was facing drought, a group of farmers in Maharashtra, who could not remember when they had had their last good meal, were closely watching the news in the only village home that had a television. They were tired not from working in the fields but from waiting for the rains. They were aware that at this late juncture, even if it rained, the crop yield would only be a fraction of what they'd hoped for, or none at all. Four farmers from the village had killed themselves in the last few weeks. The others watched the television with eyes as dry and parched as the land, feeling as powerless as the emaciated children on the screen. Silently they watched their own story being told to them by a man in a suit and tie. A woman broke into quiet sobs. But soon there was a commercial break, with advertisements for shampoo, cars and pizza oozing with cheese. This was followed by the next big news item—a wedding reception held in Mumbai. The bride was the daughter of a government minister, the groom the son of an industrialist with a business empire in petrochemicals, infrastructure and mining. The opulence of the wedding was on full display. The woman who had been sobbing quietly stood up. She picked up a small earthen pot nearby and hurled it at the television screen. Others in the room stood up and watched her in silence as someone switched off the television. They all returned to their own houses, but no one slept that night.

In the morning, one of the men from the village, who happened to be a part of Vikram's network, told him it was time to act on their plan. Vikram spread the word and sent messages to the set of contacts who were the prinicipal nodes in his database. They in turn sent messages to people in their own list and so on, until all the people in villages, towns and cities received the message. They also informed the

police and permission was sought for a peaceful march and
assembly in the Azad maidan in Mumbai, and several parks
and maidans in all the towns and cities across the country.
Nobody had envisaged the scale of the march. Nobody had
expected that everything would come to a complete halt.

Within six days, the villagers started to walk or take
bus rides to the nearest railway station and board trains to
Mumbai. Word got around to other villages, districts, and
across states. *It is time, six days from now.* That was the
message. They had often talked about doing this and had
been eagerly anticipating it. All over the country, the poor
left their villages and started moving towards the cities, to all
the state capitals. Vikram informed Trevor and Mallika, his
principal contacts in Mumbai that they will be at the Azad
maidan. Trevor and Mallika contacted many others within
the city who had joined the network, many of whom were
students, social workers and young professionals. Trevor
also contacted people who formed a hidden majority of
the network—the men and women who lived in Mumbai's
innumerable slums and shanties. People who earned their
living as workers in small factories, mills, meat shops, metal
works, car repair, those selling goods in small matchbox-sized
shops, domestic helps, nurses, autorickshaw and taxi drivers.

And that is how Mumbai stopped as the trains, buses,
and every available space on the roads were occupied by
people. Those people in the city who had not yet left their
homes for work stayed put. But those who were on their
way to work or school or the market, were left stranded
wherever they happened to be and stood bewildered, unable
to fully fathom the implications of this new development.
The city had come to a halt many a times owing to rains

flooding the roads and railway tracks, riots, or strikes like the one organized three weeks ago.

But this was different. This was unusual. These people were on a silent march. A long march. There were so many of them that the authorities could take no action. Invisible to this world when tucked away in their villages, these people and their silent distress had now come into the midst of city life, its streets, restaurants and coffee-shops, the drawing rooms of the middle-classes and the rich. They slept there through the night as groups reached the city until the morning. A majority of the people spent the few hours of the night in parks, playgrounds and maidans until day-break.

There was no question of dispersing such a massive gathering with a lathi-charge or shelling tear gas, for they were simply occupying the spaces; there had been no violence. It did not seem like they would return to their towns and villages unless the government spoke to their leaders and convinced them that something would be done to address their grievances. There was no time to form committees, delay decisions, or resort to any of the usual ploys to deal with such critical situations. It was an administrative and logistical nightmare that couldn't be solved with political manoeuvring. What were they to do? The government in Delhi was getting reports from all over the country. All state governments were facing the same situation. An emergency cabinet meeting was called. But who would preside? The Prime Minister was in New York at a United Nations assembly meeting; the Finance Minister and a large entourage of planners and economists were away in Davos for the annual World Business Meet. The Home Minister was campaigning for a by-election in his home state in the south. The Agriculture Minister was in South Africa to chair a meeting of the International Cricket Association. The Defence Minister was in hospital, getting treatment for a spine injury.

Discussions and debates raged on television and special editions of newspapers rolled out of printing presses. Television news anchors repeatedly posed the question: Why did the government not anticipate this? Forgetting that until the most recent drought situation, they themselves had not given the rural populace the news coverage they deserved.

The Chief Minister of Maharashtra and his ministers huddled together in Mantralaya. Gulabrao Jagtap, the Water Resources Minister was among them. He watched as a television reporter questioned the people occupying the streets.

'Why are you here? What would you like to tell the government?'

'Speak to our leader,' they all said.

'Who is their leader?' asked the Chief Minister.

'Someone called Vikram Sonare from Wardha district,' said Gulabrao.

'What is his background? Which party is backing him?'

'No known affiliation. His father was a farmer who committed suicide about two years ago.'

'Let's get him here to talk.'

Two officials went out to the Azad maidan where the leader of the group was expected to be present. They found Vikram, surrounded by a group of young men who were singing and dancing in a circle. The song was a mix of Hindi, Marathi, and local slang; the words coming out clearly:

'We want our rightful share from the basket of golden
     eggs,
If you don't give it to us, we know how to snatch it
     ourselves.'

As the crowd of people made way for the two officials,
Vikram signalled to the performers. They stopped singing
and stood around him.

'We want to speak to the leader here,' declared the
officials. 'Er…Vikram Sonare?'

'Yes, I'm Vikram Sonare.'

'We would like you to come with us to the Mantralaya.
The leaders would like to discuss your problems and reach
a solution.'

Vikram spread his hand to include Mallika, Trevor, and
the group of other men and women with him. Sriram was
not among them.

'I am not alone. These are my colleagues.'

'Maybe up to five of them can accompany you.'

'No, we are not going with you. Any talking that needs
to be done will happen here.'

'What you are suggesting is impossible, ridiculous even.
Do you think the government will come here to talk to you?'

Mallika, who was standing next to Vikram, asked,
'What do you think?'

The officials went away and the singers in the group
cheered and returned to their song with a renewed gusto.

Back in Mantralaya, one minister declared that the
Chief Minister should not step outside to speak to these
people. Others agreed.

Gulabrao addressed the Chief Minister: 'Sir, if it is
acceptable to you, I can go and talk to those people.'

It was early afternoon when Gulabrao, his PA and the two officials who had met with the group earlier reached Azad maidan. After introductions, Gulabrao asked in a direct manner, 'What are your grievances?'

'The time to talk about grievances has gone, some years ago. We have demands, not grievances.'

'Everyone knows what you want. You want all your loans to be written off. We have done that before.'

'If you are so sure of what we want, then why are you here?' Vikram shot back.

'Hmm. Okay. I'm ready to listen. Tell me what your demands are. Remember, I'm only listening, there are no promises.'

The people sitting behind Vikram chanted, 'Promises, promises! Now they are not even making promises!'

Vikram and the rest of the group sat cross-legged on the ground. Gulabrao's PA helped him lower his bulk to face them and the others were forced to follow suit, while their security men stood and scanned the crowd for suspicious movements.

Vikram thought for a moment and began, 'Minister...'

Gulabrao cringed. The absence of 'Honourable' was conspicuous, but he ignored it.

'Minister, all of us here from the villages are directly, or indirectly, connected to farming. We grow food for the nation. But to have food on our own plates is getting more and more difficult with each passing year. And this is not just because of the lack of rains—the policies that have been made and followed have been such that all odds are set against us. We cannot afford to buy the materials that are required for farming: seed, fertilizers, pesticides. We are forced to sell our produce to the government at whatever price they determine. And in return what life do we have? No proper schools, hospitals, or any recreational facilities. Not only that, we are just barely able to subsist on such little food; that is, when we can afford it. The rest of the time, we go hungry. When we do eat, we eat less than what our bodies need. We are no more masters of our own lives. And if we decide to migrate for work to the cities, what life awaits us here? Our homes will be in slums that smell of the gutter. We will have to queue up each morning for water and even for toilets. At least in the village we have fresh air. What will we have here? Matchbox-sized homes in which we will live like cockroaches. Our plates will still not hold enough with the rising prices, while your plate will get fuller and fuller, and overflow with food. Your bank lockers and hidden safes are filled with money. You have not one but many large homes. If you become unwell, you have the best facilities available, which you can easily afford, or better still, you can go abroad for a treatment holiday!'

'That is quite a long lecture. Come to the point, what are your demands?' said Gulabrao, impatiently.

'We are not interested in working like slaves in the city. We want to work on our own farms with the same kinds of facilities and concessions that are given to manufacturing and other industries. We want all basic facilities to be provided as an "incentive" to work in agriculture. We want action to be taken for this within two months.'

'Or else what?'

'We will stop working.'

'What do you mean by that?'

'We will go on strike. No sowing will be done. No cotton, no grains. No rice, wheat, or pulses. No vegetables or fruit trees.'

Gulabrao pushed back the sleeves of his white kurta and laughed but immediately checked himself, looking serious again.

'You cannot do that. What will you survive on?'

'We will grow food only for ourselves. As far as the government is concerned, we are on an indefinite strike from all farming work. All work will be stopped indefinitely.'

Back in Mantralaya, the Chief Minister told Gulabrao and the other ministers, 'We should prepare a statement and tell them that action will be taken to address their issues. A committee of four ministers and two officials will be formed. It will take up the matter for discussion and create a plan within two months. Let us finish this within the next hour and a half. I have an important meeting at the Grand Hyatt with a business delegation from Canada.'

'But sir, the roads are blocked. It will not be easy to go there from here.'

'What do you mean by "not easy"? I am the Chief Minister. This is my state and my city. I will fly there if I have to.'

'Yes, sir. A helicopter would be the best option.'

The Chief Minister rattled a few more orders.

'I will read out a statement to the media and Gulabrao will meet those people again. Get them moving out of the city before evening and put them onto outgoing trains. Let there be special trains for this. It will be too dangerous to have them crawling around the city at night.'

Gulabrao went back to the maidan with his team and spoke to Vikram and the others. As the sun began to set that evening, most of the streets were cleared of people and movement of vehicles stirred back to normal bit by bit.

24

THE MOVEMENT

A full year of activities, meetings, membership registrations and preliminary elections amongst the people transformed the nascent 'new co-operative movement' into a political party. Simply called the Democratic Citizens Party, the first elections that the party members stood for were the village and district councils and the municipal elections in towns and cities. Their unique strategy was to campaign through community activities that involved party members interacting directly with the people. The party did not put up posters or ads in newspapers or on televisions to spread its message. Instead, door-to-door campaigning, text messages, emails and social media were put to their fullest use.

At the first conclave of the newly formed Democratic Citizens Party, the venue was packed to capacity. The party had gathered in a huge tent at Azad maidan in Mumbai. The top was covered in cloth of many colours and people sat on the ground on rough cotton and jute durries. The founders of the party were on the dais, also sitting cross-legged on the floor. The tent was stark and clean, no buntings, flowers or garlands decorating the space. The animated crowd suddenly fell silent when Vikram picked up the microphone. He had prepared a speech the previous night but now spoke without referring to any paper. To the audience, he appeared to be speaking straight from his heart.

On stage, Vikram looked serene and older than his twenty-four years. His eyes swept through the entire gathering before he started to speak.

'Friends,' he addressed the committee members and the audience.

'Friends, I will not thank you all for coming here in large numbers. We are all in this together, equal in our passion and spirit to meet our goals for a free, progressive, and most importantly, peaceful and secure society in our great nation. It is important to understand that we want to build a new society that is free of cruelty and corruption, is based on fairness, honesty and transparency. We are all here because we believe in this cause and we want to be a part of it.

'We are all conscious of our limitations. Nobody is perfect. But with our sincerity, hard work and passion towards the cause, we will certainly strive to achieve our goals. To truly achieve our goals, we must bring together the people dwelling in villages and cities. This can happen only if our villages are modernized without losing their ethos and without damaging or violating the sanctity of the environment or rural life, of which we are the sole representatives. Basic necessities of life must be available in all villages, especially to farmers and labourers. Without their hard work there will be no food for any of us in this country. Friends, let us talk about this important issue. What would happen if the kitchens in our homes suddenly went missing? The idea is unimaginable. But that is what will happen if we neglect our farmers and our agriculture. Their work must be recognized and rewarded in the same way as all other work. We need the facilities that will allow people to not just subsist on agriculture but to live a better quality of life. To reach our goals we must stay together at all times.

'The important point is, how are we going to be different from the other political parties? Why should any citizen of India give us his or her vote? These are the most important questions that we must answer. Our understanding and our thinking must percolate down to every person in our organization. Essential to our vision is the most important rule: we must be democratic in all our decisions. All positions must be filled through a transparent process of democratic election. We will not stand for nepotism, favouritism, or any other "isms" that plague our political system today. We will not cobble up a party of power-hungry people who wish to plunder our nation under the guise of "ruling the country". Our organization should be a microcosm of the nation we wish to serve.

'Most of you would have heard the saying, "Poverty is the worst form of violence." We will strive to eradicate poverty by providing entrepreneurial opportunities to those who want to start and grow small businesses. Trade and commerce is necessary for the market to grow and a profit must be made for businesses to be viable, but not at the cost of impoverishing others.

'In the quest to reach our common goal of forming a political party, I have met and interacted with many people. They represent the emerging face of our country—social and business entrepreneurs, activists and journalists, teachers, civil servants, lawyers, and honest citizens pursuing their livelihoods—who are willing to spare their time in service of the nation. Some of them are the women and men you see seated here with me on the dais. Please understand that all of you sitting in the audience are equally important members of this new movement and will be given a chance to speak, voice your opinion, and bring forth the social, cultural and political issues that you wish to address and that you think are important for our party. Thank you.'

The applause continued to resonate for a very long time.

Three more speeches followed from other members of the party's foundation committee, followed by an open discussion where those who wished to speak on a particular topic could do so without hesitation. A microphone was passed around to every hand raised. Then Mallika, the last of the party foundation committee, stood up and faced the audience.

'I want to begin by addressing the issue of the disconnect of people from politics. I think, we must involve people much more in the running of our country, not just during elections. Only then can we evolve into a new democracy that is based on our own values and is developed for our times. It is time we do that and move away from established political thought. It is time we bring freshness in our approach to daily governance.

'What essentially is our ideology? It is the very set of beliefs that are the foundation of this party. That we are all equal no matter our gender, religion, caste, class, or language. But ideology can serve its purpose only when it furthers the work of improving the lives of all citizens. It is not a sacred entity to be worshipped or used for stirring animosity between people. It must constantly evolve. It cannot remain tied to a particular person, a set of ideas or an isolated event in history. It must be forward-looking, never dogmatic or straitjacketed. And for that the involvement of people and communities is essential.

'Women are hugely outnumbered by men in politics. That will not happen in this party. If we believe in equality, it must reflect in how our party functions. This is very important for us and for our country. By our way of functioning and behaviour, we must force other parties to follow these principles of equality.'

A slew of ideas followed as more people spoke out. One amongst them was a timid-looking man, probably in his late twenties:

'I believe that the gap between rural and urban ways of life cannot be completely bridged because, they are in a way, two separate worlds. But the countryside requires not just basic infrastructure that is a given in the cities; some of the aspects of urban living must be included in the rural areas. In our country, education—particularly higher education—is accessible only in the urban areas. This has to change drastically. Why should an agriculture college be located in a city when the need for it is in the villages? Centres of engineering and commerce must also be present in villages. Penetration of higher education and medical facilities will certainly raise the rural standards of living.

'I have a vision for a set of villages that are well connected by roads and accessible by state transport buses. A village market and a tourist village could be juxtaposed so that they go hand in hand to create wealth and employment for the rural population. Education can be accessible to everyone if we realize that English need not be an excuse for us to exclude our own languages. I come from a village in Madhya Pradesh. All my life I have spoken Hindi, I still do. But to get my engineering degree, I have to learn from English books. It is a different matter that I am fluent in English. But my Hindi is better. I am sure the same holds true for many others here who are fluent in English but are more comfortable in the language they speak at home. Why can't we build knowledge in our own languages? We have a national institute that specializes in language fonts and language software. We have a pool of the most brilliant engineering and technology guys in the world who help solve the most complex problems in the developed world. Why can't we use this talent to create a new educational world that is accessible to every villager? Let a fifty-year-old farmer learn economics or physics. Who knows, he might do well and run a school in the village.

'If we do this, we can give a fair opportunity to the farmers to do something other than farming or manual labour. I mean, I hear about the "rural employment schemes"—and what is offered to farmers, whose farms are not giving them enough? Digging and construction jobs to build roads? I don't mean to suggest that manual work is not required or is less important. But is that all we have to offer? Can we not create better opportunities, offer better choices that will improve their lives? We have to create a new world in our villages.'

And so, it was on the day of the conclave, after all the speeches and discussions were over at five in the evening, all the members of the Democratic Citizens Party, from rural and urban India, took an oath to serve the common interests of the nation.

Some of the smaller regional parties began to lose popularity, while the major political parties tried to reinvent themselves with the old tried-and-tested methods. Television celebrities and filmstars were the first people they brought in to woo more voters. But the ideology of the Democratic Citizens Party had caught the imagination of the people. The television news channels had begun to call these new entrants for interviews and covered them extensively. Viewers and readers had begun to show a genuine interest in discovering new people from far-flung parts of the country. At first they were a novelty, but gradually they gained respect as fellow citizens whose passionate views were heard seriously and discussed in every public forum.

It was extraordinary to witness how such large numbers of people, leading ordinary lives, were willing to put themselves on the path of political empowerment. And yet, it was the most natural thing to have happened. A group of journalists started up a new YouTube channel titled *Real India*. They invited people from all strata of society to participate in discussions rather than limiting debate to the same set of 'opinion makers'. They travelled to different villages and towns to speak to all sorts of people in their interactive programmes.

A group of college students, taking a cue from one of the speeches at the conclave, formed a small start-up that would bring higher education to the rural areas through vernacular languages. This huge project involved the translation and creation of knowledge bases in all Indian languages. 'Why should English be a precondition for higher education?' they asked. They promised to bring education, in a true and complete sense, to the villages so that people there could work and live better lives without the need to migrate to cities to supplement their incomes from farm work. Why should a village have to import teachers and doctors from the cities? Why not nurture them in the villages?

While more and more people were coming forward to join the Party of their own volition, others who could contribute their experience and knowledge were also invited. Mallika asked Bhaskar Prabhu to join the party, but he declined: 'I cannot be a part of any political party. I will continue to work as a reporter.'

In Wardha, Vikram met Manoj Rathod and invited him to join the party. He, too, declined. 'I will work with farmers as part of the Farmers' Association. But from my past experience, I prefer to stay away from politics and politicians.'

'Past experience?'

'Yes. There was a time when a friend, a member of our association, joined a political party. In fact, he was our leader. But when we were protesting against a government policy that forced us to buy seeds from the Queen Seeds and Agroseeds conglomerate, it was the leader who betrayed our cause and sold us out to the government.'

'How is it that I don't know about this?'

'Oh, you were probably very young at the time, a toddler, and such things are often buried under the carpet. But, anyway, I wish you the very best. And remember... while you build your new political party, the other parties are not going to just stand aside and watch you succeed. They will not let go of power so easily, not without putting up a very strong fight. They will use foul means to thwart your efforts. So be warned!'

Bhaskar Prabhu, Manoj Rathod, Dr Kabir Ahmed and Vikram's mother, Kashibai Sonare, were the four people who formed the advisory panel for the movement and the political party. Other prominent people joined this panel gradually over several months.

25

A NEW COMMITMENT

While the new party gathered strength over the course of a year, Gulabrao's clout in the INP was also on the rise. Rumours persisted that a faction of legislators led by him planned to rebel against the Chief Minister of Maharashtra. His ambition to occupy the chair was well known in political circles, and discontented members of other parties had been in touch with him to form a new alliance. But when news of these developments reached the INP party president, Gulabrao Jagtap was summoned to Delhi. After several deliberations and a reshuffling of the Central Government, he was sworn in as the new Minister of Power, making him part of the Prime Minister's cabinet. But he was also given an unofficial assignment by the party president: to inveigle the leaders of the new people's movement and thwart the formation of their political party.

Through his friend Uday Dhanraj, Gulabrao had been in touch with Sriram Kasbekar who had conducted a padayatra across the country, which included Vikram Sonare, the leader of the people's movement. He secretly congratulated himself for his own foresight in taking the initiative to talk to them during that crisis in Mumbai. He thought it would be difficult to manipulate Vikram Sonare, but Dr Sriram Kasbekar would be an easier target.

It was no surprise then that Dhanraj Industries instituted a new award and conferred it on Kasbekar, who received it with some humility and much pleasure. It was not something he had ever wanted or craved for. But Sriram could not wait for the day of the award function. He had left the people's movement that Mallika and Vikram had got involved in. It seemed too impractical and full of uncertainties. The award function was to take place on the same day that Vikram and Mallika were to address the first political rally of the Democratic Citizens Party in Mumbai, a year after the first conclave.

After the award function, Uday Dhanraj told Sriram about his plan to form a trust that would lay the foundation of a social service organization. He invited Sriram to be the chairman of this new entity, but since Sriram had already parted ways with the new political movement, this strategy was useless. So, Gulabrao now tried other, more direct methods to attack the new party.

Meanwhile, at the rally, Vikram stood up to take the floor, with loud applause from the crowd. But amid the roar, a stone was hurled towards the stage. It hit Vikram on the shoulder. More stones flew through the air as the on-duty policemen moved in to catch the offenders in the audience. Onstage, a party member asked the people to remain calm.

But another barrage of stones came pelting down onto the stage, along with larger rocks being hurled at the audience. Amidst cries of pain and panic, the crowd swirled in all directions, breaking the bamboo barricades as they tried to flee.

Party volunteers and the police struggled to contain the crowd, people bolted and ran, crashing into one another. In the confusion, Mallika spotted Sudha trying to catch her attention from the periphery of the stage. As she reached her, Sudha grabbed Mallika's wrist and pulled her out of the crowd and onto the road, pushing her behind a car parked along the street. As she followed Mallika behind the car, a stone hurled from the other side of the road hit her on the head and she fell. Mallika tried to reach her but was trapped in the gap between the car and the footpath for the next several minutes, as hordes of people thundered past in a mad frenzy. When the pandemonium subsided, she rushed to Sudha. Her reddened face was almost unrecognizable. One of her eyes was closed, while the other was smeared in blood.

Once the crowd was brought under control, ambulances rushed to the site to attend to the injured people. Sudha and another party worker were taken to the hospital. As Mallika sat at Sudha's feet in the ambulance, all their interactions flashed through her mind. She remembered the time when she sat on the side of the road with Iyer's corpse wrapped in a white sheet next to her. As they brought Sudha into the hospital's emergency ward, Vikram also arrived and Mallika began to cry. Sudha was carried on a stretcher into the operation theatre. Vikram and Mallika sat on the bench outside and waited.

An hour later, they were told that the patient was alright. The injuries were not critical and the wound had been stitched up. But they wanted to keep Sudha under observation for another day. Vikram and Mallika went into the ward and waited by Sudha's bed.

Mallika couldn't stop her eyes from welling up. Vikram said, almost inaudibly, 'Maybe this was not a good idea. Maybe there are other ways.'

Mallika wiped her eyes.

'No, Vikram. Never say that. This is just the beginning. We have to be strong, stronger than we are now. We have to be ready for violence. If one of us falls, there will be another to take her place. Never doubt what you have started.'

'What *we* have started.'

'Yes, Vikram, what we have started.'

Those words sealed the bond between them. A bond that had been growing stronger ever since they began working together. They knew they had to stick together for this radical new movement to succeed. And that if they did succeed, it would change the fate of the nation.

Sudha opened her eyes and whispered, 'She is right you know. This is just the beginning.'

EPILOGUE

When the general elections were held at the beginning of summer, Mallika and Vikram hoped that their party would win enough seats to make their voice heard in Parliament. It was their first attempt, and although the party cadre had great hopes, the leaders were pragmatic. Seven first-time members of the new Democratic Citizens Party were elected into the Parliament. Mallika, elected from Central Mumbai, was among them. So was Vikram Sonare, the leader of the party. Their real work has only just begun. The fact that they are in Opposition only makes it more challenging.

The people of Sonsawali village were jubilant but finding it hard to believe that a young man from their village, a farmer's son, was soon going to be sworn-in as a Member of Parliament. Through him, their voice would be heard in the nation's capital.

That summer, a new enthusiasm infused the farmers in Sonsawali village as they cultivated their fields. It was their hard work, their election, their candidates, and now their own man in Parliament. After the sowing, they eagerly waited to reap the fruits of their toil. They were used to waiting each year for the monsoon. It was the same this year too. It seemed as if it would never rain. But they waited a bit longer...through the smouldering heat, through the stewing nights with a vague promise of a hint of breeze that never actually arrived.

On a day when hope was at an end, a little girl laughed in delight when the very first raindrop fell on her cheek. And then it rained. It rained and rained and rained. The showers soaked the clothes of the men, women and children, who danced in the fields and on the dirt roads that became slushy with mud.

Some days later that same little girl found in the field a tiny white stalk that had emerged and a small green leaf was sticking out at the tip of the seedling.

ACKNOWLEDGEMENTS

This book would not have been possible without the inspiration and encouragement of P. Sainath. He opened for me the world of rural India and the agrarian crisis in a way that nobody else could have done.

I'm grateful for the invaluable help during my research for this book to Jaideep Hardikar, Vijay Jawandhia, Kamlabai Gudhe and her family, Anil Shidore and Makarand Sahasrabuddhe.

My sincere thanks to Namita Gokhale, Vikram Chandra, Nilanjana Roy, Vijaya Madhavan, Arvind Kher, Balaji Ratnam, Anjan Mukherjee, Will Davis, Beth McMillan, Amit Wamburkar, Aparna Karthikeyan, Thejaswi Puthraya, Meenal Sahoo, Lavanya-Shanbogue Arvind, Suraksha Giri and Sujatha Giri for their support in so many ways.

I thank Ravi Singh for giving a home to this book; Radhika Shenoy, my patient editor and friend; the team at Speaking Tiger for bringing out this book; and my agent Preeti Gill, for her timely help.

I am ever grateful to my father Shailendra Moghe and my mother, the Late Sushma Moghe, for bringing books into our lives and sparking the joy of reading in me. I thank my brothers Sunil and Jayant and their families for their love and support.

I feel blessed and am grateful to my daughter Advaita, my most sincere critic, and to my husband Makarand Waikar for his unstinted support in everything I do.